IN THE COUNTRY IN THE DARK

IN THE COUNTRY IN THE DARK

DARYL SNEATH

DOUG WHITEWAY, EDITOR

Signature
EDITIONS

Cover design by Doowah Design.
Photo of Daryl Sneath by Penelope & Abigael Sneath

This book was printed on Ancient Forest Friendly paper.
Printed and bound in Canada by Hignell Book Printing Inc.

We acknowledge the support of the Canada Council for the Arts and the Manitoba Arts Council for our publishing program.

Library and Archives Canada Cataloguing in Publication

Title: In the country in the dark / Daryl Sneath ; Doug Whiteway, editor.
Names: Sneath, Daryl, 1975- author. | Whiteway, Doug, 1951- editor.
Identifiers: Canadiana (print) 20230464122 |
Canadiana (ebook) 20230464130 |
ISBN 9781773241234 (softcover) |
ISBN 9781773241241 (EPUB)
Subjects: LCGFT: Novels.
Classification: LCC PS8637.N43 I52 2023 | DDC C813/.6—dc23

Signature Editions
P.O. Box 206, RPO Corydon, Winnipeg, Manitoba, R3M 3S7
www.signature-editions.com

If there was one thing responsible
for ruining lives, it was love.

— Heather O'Neill

TWO CUPS

—◆◆◆—

Joy Kalm, twenty-eight, and Landon Wood, thirty-three, met in Naturalis, an upscale downtown furniture and craft store. Landon was there to pick up a cheque. He was a freelance woodworker. The store was one of his main clients. Joy happened to be strolling by the storefront, hands in her back pockets, a little smile in her eyes for what she assessed to be the perfect balance of light and cloud in the sky, when a short man in a long coat threw open the door like he meant to break free. He managed to dodge Joy but not by much. Looking up the sidewalk, then down, he mumbled something and fled, long coat trailing him like a cape. Joy tucked her hair and watched him go. She watched the door close, too, which took a few seconds. Engineered, no doubt, for safety and grace. There was a faint click when the door finally came shut and Joy waited. No one came running after the short man in the long coat. She laughed a little. She hoped he had made off with a bit of treasure. Joy imagined painting him. She gave him a pipe and dark eyes and a smirk. She captured the speed of his fleeing in the flutter of his long coat. She thought of a title: *The Artful Dodger*.

The sun burst through the clouds and glinted off the glass door. Joy squinted and when the clouds shuttered the sun again, her eyes settled on the store's name. She read it as "Natural is." She wanted to ask someone, Natural is what? On the store-wide window beside the door two more words were stamped in cursive white: *Imagine. Experience.* She smiled and tucked her hair. In the window, behind the words, there was a plush designer armchair and a standing lamp. She could not afford either but imagined sitting in the chair while reading under the light of the lamp and drinking indefensibly expensive wine.

Always on the lookout for a little adventure, Joy pulled the heavy silver handle and entered the store. Perhaps she would find a little treasure herself.

—◆—

Staring at his name stamped in the middle of the small white envelope, as though the envelope were a map he was holding and his own name identified the destination, Landon made his measured way from the back of the store to the front along exactly the same path he had taken on his way in. Joy was standing near the entrance, which was also the exit, and she was thinking about this dichotomy when she took a hand-carved canoe from a glass shelf and turned it in her hands. She felt something holding it. She thought about taking it. Landon did not see Joy standing there. When he bumped into her she fumbled the canoe and he dropped the envelope. With a quick hand Landon caught the canoe and looked at it. It was a piece, he noticed, that he had made.

"Forgive me," he said.

Joy bent to pick up the envelope and handed it to Landon. He took it and nodded once and returned the canoe to the shelf. He adjusted the bow of the little boat so that it made a perfect forty-five-degree angle with the glass edge, as if it were pointed upstream and ferrying across the width of a glass river. The sight of it pleased him.

"That's a bit extreme," Joy said.

He thought she meant what he had done with the canoe. He looked at her.

She smiled and tucked her hair. "But if you insist." She pretended to touch his shoulder with a wand. "You are forgiven."

The artist in her took note of what she saw. His eyes were ice-blue, hooded by a serious brow, though the man behind the eyes, she quickly assessed, was unaware how serious. His nose and chin were strong and prominent and proportional. She imagined painting him. A title came to her: *Man, Forgiven.*

Landon did not have an artist's sensibilities but he did notice three specific things about Joy. One, her green eyes. Two, her hair, which fell past her shoulders and had a single braid like a thin rope within it. He did not know what to call the colour of her hair but it reminded him of the colour of the antique pine furniture he had inherited from his parents. And three, how small she was. Not short but wisp thin. He could lift her from the ground with one arm around her waist and hold her there against him forever.

She held out her hand. "My name is Joy."

Landon looked at the name on the clean white page in his mind.

Joy.

He took her hand in his and told himself not to hold it for too long.

"I like that name. It suits you."

"I'm not sure how you would know that," she said, smiling again. "We've only just met."

Landon set a finger to his lips. It looked, Joy thought, like he was shushing someone, or like he was in contemplation.

"Do you like coffee?"

"Yes," she said. "I do."

"Do you actually like it? A lot of people want to like it. A lot of people say they like it. A lot of people drink it and pretend to like it even though all they really like is the smell or the effect or the ritual. Or some combination of the three."

"No. I like coffee exceedingly."

Landon looked puzzled.

"It's a line. From Lovecraft."

Landon thought about the word Lovecraft. It reminded him of witchcraft.

It was clear to Joy he had no idea what she meant. "The writer."

"Oh. I don't read much."

"Well—"

She smiled for the third time. Landon had counted.

"—I do. And I like coffee. Exceedingly."

"There's a shop next door called The Pinecone Café. The barista there pulls the finest espresso I have ever had. I would like to buy you one."

"You don't look like someone who uses words like *barista*." She tilted her head at him. "You don't look like someone who drinks espresso."

Landon thought about what Joy said.

She hugged herself. "I'm not sure why I said that."

"People usually say things because they think them."

Joy took Landon by the hand. "If it's the finest espresso you have ever had," she said, "I would like to buy *you* one."

—◆—

Behind the counter the barista—sporting a tiny silver skull in her nose and pixie-cut, silk-green hair—ground and collected and tamped the coffee beans, which, for people who like espresso, was entertaining and fully part of the experience.

The barista reminded Joy of Victoria. Victoria had worn her hair short, too, when Joy knew her, and changed the colour every Sunday while she washed the sheets and pinned them to the rail of the balcony to dry in the southern Vancouver Island air. Victoria's hair was bubblegum pink when Joy met her, then purple, then blue, then silver, then candy-apple red. Instead of a nose ring, Victoria had a lip ring, and when she thought about it Joy could still feel the cold metal of that ring on her own lips. She sketched Victoria's lips in Victoria's sketchbook without Victoria knowing. The lips took up a whole page. Joy had tried to make the lips look as soft as they were in life. She imagined

Victoria finding the sketch. She imagined her carefully cutting the sketch from the book, folding the page into a paper plane, and tossing it off the balcony, touching her actual lips as she watched the folded sketch of her lips fall and glide away. She imagined Victoria blowing the plane a kiss as though the plane were Joy herself. Joy saw all of this in an instant in her head. She told herself she would paint the sketch of Victoria's lips one day. A title occurred to her: *Parted Lips, Sweet Sorrow.*

The barista set the two espressos on the counter and smiled when she did.

Joy returned the smile and thanked her.

Landon looked at Joy and then he looked at the barista and thanked her in kind. He could not remember if he had ever thanked her before and it bothered him. That he could not remember. And that he might not have thanked her.

The two armchairs by the fireplace were empty and so Landon and Joy sat in them. The way Landon's chair felt reminded him of the chair he had sat in all those afternoons in that office where the man who wore sweaters sat behind a desk and asked him questions and encouraged him to talk and took notes when he did. Landon looked at Joy and wondered if she liked the chair she was sitting in. He wondered if something like a chair would ever trigger for her some past comfort she wished she could revisit or share, like him. He wondered what she was thinking.

Accomplished amateur paintings—cityscapes and landscapes—hung on the exposed-brick wall by the fireplace. The largest of the collection sat on an easel. Landon stared at it for a while and Joy watched him. In the foreground of the painting the artist had featured a barn, dilapidated and abandoned. A red wheelbarrow (which reminded Joy of the poem) rested on its side by an empty coop. The coop had a little wooden sign driven into the ground in front of it. Above the barn, like a dream, the image of a city pressing down upon it. In the sky above the image of the city, a god-like figure: bearded, hair blown to one side, bare-chested, physically robust. The title of the painting, written on a price tag shaped like an oversized coffee mug, read *The Modern of Time.*

"I like that painting."

Joy nodded. She found it garish. "What do you like about it?"

"The barn."

"If that painting were the first in a series the barn would no longer exist by the end."

"I know. I see it disappearing. I think that's part of what I like."

"That says a lot about you—that you like diminishing things."

Landon thought about the phrase *diminishing things*. "If I could somehow remove the image of the city and that god in the sky I could save the barn."

Joy clapped her hands together once. "I say you do it. I'll ask for a brush and a palette of blues."

Landon looked confused. He didn't know if she was serious. "I don't think I could do that."

"Why not?"

Joy fixed her eyes on his and he could not look away.

"For one, I can't paint."

"Anybody can paint."

Landon looked at her with a serious expression. "No. I don't think so. I don't think that's true."

"It can't be that hard."

Landon caught himself looking at Joy's lips as she spoke. He wanted to touch them.

Joy finished her coffee and looked at the bottom of the cup, which held a few grounds. There were people, she thought, who saw the future in such remains. She would love to know what future was in these remains.

She looked at the painting. "I like the easel."

The easel looked to Landon like it had been built from a kit. He found it simple and forgettable.

"What do you like about it?"

"The colour and the grain. The simplicity. It's there to hold the painting and nothing more. It's okay with going unnoticed."

"Do you know where the word *easel* comes from?"

"No." She settled her hands in her lap and leaned forward. "But I'd like to."

"It comes from the Dutch, *ezel*. Which means ass. The beast of burden." He shrugged. "I don't know why I know that."

"I don't know that anyone knows why they know anything."

Landon liked the way Joy said things. It would be, he decided, the first thing about her he loved.

The song in the background ended and a new one began. Landon recognized it immediately. Johnny Cash doing the old folk tune "Run On For a Long Time." He would like to take Joy home and play this song for her on the record player he had inherited from his mother. In addition to the record player, his mother had given him many things: the wave in his hair, the blueness of his eyes, his love of music. His father had passed things on, too: a physical heft and a gentle demeanour that seemed at odds with one another, attention to detail, a talent with wood and a level of patience to nurture that talent. They had been good parents. They had been a happy family. He saw the word *family* on the clean white page in his mind. It had been so long since it had been anything other than a word.

When the song was over Joy set her cup on the table between them. She wondered what he was thinking. "Let's do this again."

Landon took a deep breath and held it. He set his own cup beside hers on the table between them. He turned the cup like it was the dial on a lock: clockwise, then counter, then clockwise again. When he finished, he took his hand away and looked at the cups. The handles were almost touching.

She watched him.

Eventually Landon looked up. When he did he told himself to be sure to make eye contact. Eye contact, the man who wore sweaters had told him, was essential.

"Yes," Landon said. "Let's."

Joy, in her journal

His eyes are like blue glass shot through with
the sun. There's a gentleness about him and an
earnestness I'm not sure he's aware of. What he
said about the barn in the painting was peculiar.
I liked it. And that thing he did with the cups, the
way he brought the handle of his to within a hair
of mine. Strange he didn't tell me his name. But
also kind of wonderful.

Landon, not quite to himself

I babbled a bit about the coffee and the painting.

I wouldn't worry.

I always worry.

Deep breaths.

Her eyes—what colour are they?

Green.

There must be a more specific word. And her hair. It's like antique furniture.

I wouldn't tell her that.

She's beautiful.

Yes.

Beautiful's not the word either.

Yes, it is. Like green, it's clear and easy to understand.

Joy. What a perfect name.

You realize you didn't tell her yours.

I'll tell her tomorrow.

Good idea.

I love the way she speaks.

She is smart. Yes.

Smart isn't the word but I know what you mean.

Smart is the word.

I love the way she tucks her hair behind her ear. How can such a simple gesture be so—

Attractive?

More than that.

Intoxicating?

Maybe. Whatever it is I love it.

Well. I think that's enough for this session.

Probably.

Don't be early tomorrow. You don't want to seem desperate.

Good point.

Whatever you do don't mention the house in the country.

What if it comes up?

It will only come up if you bring it up.

Maybe it's fate.

There's no such thing.

She was in the store. She was looking at a canoe that I carved.

Moments in a day that happened to coincide. It means nothing.

Nothing means nothing.

Well.

There's a river by the house. I could build her a real canoe. I could carve her a paddle.

Don't say any of that to her.

I won't. And I won't mention the house in the country. Yet.

Landon went to the garage where he selected a piece of cherry the size of a brick from the material he kept organized, by size and by type, on a series of seven shelves he had made, and set about carving a canoe similar to the one Joy was looking at when he bumped into her.

When he was finished he took a cloth bag and went to the nearby park to collect ten small pinecones. Satisfied with his collection, he came home and arranged the pinecones in the canoe. Only nine fit. He put the extra one in his pocket, later placing it alongside the other pinecone he kept in the bedside table drawer. He set the canoe with nine pinecones in a box and wrapped the box with brown paper. He made a cross of green raffia (for her eyes) and tied a bow. The wrapping material came from the surplus his mother had always kept on hand. He had not wrapped a gift in a long time. He had done a fine job with it.

TIME ENOUGH

—◆◆◆—

A block away from the coffee shop Landon stopped and checked his watch (it had been his father's: silver face, Roman numerals, a worn leather band the old smell of which gave him comfort). Ten to ten. Maybe she was there already. He pictured her in the chair by the fire, explaining as he approached that she liked to be fashionably early. *Why should the late,* she might say, *have a monopoly on fashion?* He would sit and say something about the word *monopoly,* how he'd always wondered about the juxtaposition of *mono* and *poly,* whether the etymologies of the parts had something to do with the meaning of the whole or whether it was merely linguistic accident. He liked thinking about words, he'd tell her. So did she, she'd say. A conversation would begin.

A hand touched his shoulder. He turned.

Joy smiled and tucked her hair.

He said her name.

She was standing fairly close to him and so when he offered his hand it was only a few inches from his chest. "I'm Landon. I neglected to tell you."

She mimicked his shortened arm and took his hand in hers.

"This must've been what it was like," she said, "when one T-rex shook the hand of another."

"That's clever," he said. "You're clever."

Joy slipped both hands in the back pockets of her jeans, which made her hips come forward. Landon folded his arms.

Strangers walked by in both directions. Drivers blew their horns. An old man leaned out his apartment window and coughed. Then laughed. Maybe at the morning drunk staggering across the street proclaiming the imminent end of the world and the everlasting love of Jesus. Closer to them, a child in a daisy-patterned dress twirled round and round and round. A woman, the child's mother maybe, sat on the steps nearby and smoked. Pigeons took note from their window ledges above. The city lived on.

Landon looked at Joy. He hadn't stopped looking at her. When he realized, he said, "Forgive me."

"Again with the forgiveness."

"Sorry. It's a habit."

"Sins abound then. Bodies in the closet?"

"No." He tried a smile. He remembered what the man who wore sweaters had said about the importance of humour. "I wouldn't go in the basement though."

She feigned a shiver. "How very House of Usher of you. I like it."

He furrowed his brow.

"Right," she said. "You don't read much."

"No," he said. "I'm sorry. I don't."

"Whatever you do, don't be sorry." She poked a finger in his chest. "But we'll have to fix the not-reading much. Won't we."

He liked that she'd said *we*.

◆

They walked the block to the coffee shop. Joy kept her hands in her back pockets and Landon liked the way it made her move. He held the door for her when they arrived but decided against making it a routine. They stood in line and ordered their coffees: an Americano for Landon, a flat white for Joy. They took the empty chairs again by the fire. If they came a third time and the chairs were not empty Landon would not be able to sit anywhere else. He wondered if he should tell Joy this now or wait to see if the occasion arose. They set their cups on the table between them and watched the steam rise. In the background, William Prince sang "The Spark."

"I like her," Joy said.

Landon looked confused.

Joy gestured toward the counter. "The barista." She stopped herself from telling him about Victoria. She didn't know why. She usually said what came to mind.

"I agree. She makes a fine coffee."

"It's more than coffee," Joy said. "It's a work of art. I almost don't want to drink it." She leaned forward and admired the white design in the crema. "I love that it's a pinecone." She looked at him. "Pinecones might be my favourite thing in nature."

Landon thought of the pinecones he had collected and placed in the canoe that now sat in a box, wrapped, on the shelf in his front closet at home. He thought of the old pinecone in the drawer of his bedside table, and the new one he had placed there beside it.

Joy used both hands to cradle the cup, closed her eyes, and took a long sip.

Landon watched her.

Joy opened her eyes. Set the cup in her lap.

"It's good then."

"Good's not the word."

He took a sip of his own coffee and nodded, his mind briefly elsewhere. "This is good, too. Well. Not good, as you pointed out, but you know what I mean."

Joy tilted her head. "I don't know why people say that. *You know what I mean*. The effect is opposite to the intention."

Landon thought about what Joy said. On this point, he wasn't sure he agreed.

"If the listener really does know what the speaker means," he said, "then saying so means exactly what the speaker intends. Even if there are no other words to express what they both understand."

She pointed at him. "I like it. But you should know—and I think you do—there are always other words."

They sat without speaking for a while and drank their coffees. Landon could not remember feeling this at ease with someone, maybe ever, in his life. They listened to the music in the background. The next song, which they both recognized by the opening acoustic line and Donovan Woods's four-count, was "Put On, Cologne." Joy liked the loop about stupid European boyfriends and logical ends. It reminded her of who she had loved in Marseille and Dublin and Berlin. She started singing. She had a beautiful voice. Landon thought about telling her. When the song ended Joy came forward in her chair and put her cup on the table.

"I've noticed something strange about you."

"People usually do."

She narrowed her eyes like she was assessing something about him. "You're funny."

"No one's ever told me that before."

It was good, he thought, that she thought he was funny, but the problem, as he saw it, was that in this instance he had not intended to be. He thought about intentions and misunderstanding. The man who wore sweaters used to say that sometimes the best of the former lead to the worst of the latter and the reason often lies in our inability to look beyond ourselves. Landon told the man he tried to look beyond himself but he could never get past the paradox. Perspective is limited by each of us. No one can ever see what another person sees. True, the man said. No one ever really knows anyone, and no one ever really knows what anyone else knows, but the more we listen the closer we come. It was such a beautiful day, Landon told the man. Bad things are not supposed to happen on beautiful days. That's a perfect example of what I mean. Trying to make sense of something that resists making sense is the opposite of looking beyond. It sends us endlessly inward and we spin and we spin. Sometimes letting go is the only way out. Landon didn't think he could let go, which is why he still held on. He liked holding on. Holding on gave him comfort.

Joy watched him. She assessed him. She wondered what he was thinking.

She tapped the table with a single finger, a beat for each word she spoke. "The thing I noticed," she said, "is that you never check your phone."

"I've noticed the same thing. About you."

"That's because I don't have one. To check."

"Neither do I."

She reached across the table for his hand and touched it. "We might be the only two people on the planet."

She kept her hand on his for a moment and then took it away. She adjusted herself in the chair. Landon felt the ghost of Joy's hand on his. What she said about being the only two people on the planet reminded him of something and, deciding she might be interested, he told her about it.

"There's an episode of *The Twilight Zone* called 'Time Enough At Last.'"

"Like the poem about making the most of your time."

"That fits. The episode's about a man who loves books. He's a bank teller—"

Joy cut in. "What's it called, where a bank teller stands. Not a window."

"A wicket."

She pointed. "A wicket. Yes. Continue."

"Henry Bemis is the bank teller. He wants nothing more than to read. Every chance he gets."

"I love him already."

"At one point his wife plays a trick on him. She hands him a book and asks him to read it to her. Excited by the prospect he takes the book, but when he opens it he discovers she's inked out all the lines. The sight of a book he cannot read crushes him. Spurred on by his dismay his wife rips the volume from his hands and tears out all the pages."

"How awful," Joy said. "I hate her."

"I feel sorry for her."

"Really."

"She suffers because of his obsession."

"It doesn't sound like obsession to me. It sounds like passion."

"What's the difference?"

"Control."

"—."

Joy explained. "One is uncontrollable and ruinous. The other is purposeful suffering and often selfless."

"I should note Bemis is farsighted. Without his glasses he cannot read a word."

"I've thought about getting glasses." Joy pretended to slip a pair of glasses on and pursed her lips. "What do you think?" Before Landon could answer she removed the invisible glasses, twirled them once, and threw them away. "Better to be as I am. Unadorned."

Part of the word rose above the rest and appeared on the clean white page in Landon's mind.

Adore.

He thought of the Amy Shark song and it played in his head.

"So," Joy said. "What happens next?"

"Bemis is working at the bank one day and he takes his lunch to the vault so he can eat and read in peace. Settled, he takes up a newspaper and notices a headline about the atomic bomb. Just then, there's an explosion that knocks him unconscious. When he comes to, he discovers that the entire city has been completely devastated and he's the only person who's survived."

"Which plummets him into despair."

"At first, yes. He reacts like most people would react. In fact, he happens upon a gun and contemplates killing himself. But then he notices in the distance what's left of the library. He investigates further and finds that none of the books was destroyed in the explosion. They have, in a way, survived with him."

"Sounds like paradise."

"Paradise in hell."

Joy wrinkled her nose. "I love it."

Landon liked the way Joy wrinkled her nose. He liked the way she said I love it.

He continued: "But then something awful happens."

Joy put her hands together and touched her lips. She pointed her pressed-together hands at Landon like an arrow. "He breaks his glasses."

Landon furrowed his brow. "How did you know that?"

"It's the only possible ending."

Landon thought about what Joy said and wondered if it were true.

"I'd like to see it now," she told him.

Landon sat back in his chair. He hesitated. "I'm pretty sure I have a copy. At home, I mean."

She grinned. "By pretty sure you mean you're certain. I bet you have a boxed set. I bet it's in immaculate condition. I bet everything you own is in immaculate condition and perfectly organized."

The phrase immaculate condition made Landon think of the house in the country. The song in the background ended and a new one began. Landon looked to the speakers in the ceiling. "I like this song."

"I saw them. In Johannesburg. I was living there."

Landon had only ever lived here. Here, and the university, for those two anomalous months before the incident. And then here again.

"I've lived all over," Joy said. She thought about all the places she had lived. What took her from one place to the next. That feeling of wanting to find the thing she could not name. That need to be the one who left so that she would never again be the one who *was* left. She counted off the cities on her fingers as she named them. "Let's see. Victoria, Montreal, Marseille, Berlin, Barcelona, São Paulo, Dublin, Johannesburg, and Austin." She tucked her hair. "And now here."

"Austin." Landon said the city's name like he'd never heard it before.

"Don't ask," she said. "An actual cowboy. Biggest mistake of my life."

Landon thought that Joy must not have lived in any of these cities alone. He couldn't help but wonder about all of the love she had had in her life, and all of the love he had not.

He looked at her. He did not mean to say what he said next. He meant only to think it. Which happened sometimes. Sometimes he said out loud what he meant only to think. The man who wore sweaters told him that when this happened it was his unconscious self stepping in to make sure something meaningful did not go unsaid.

"I want to know everything there is to know about you."

Joy smiled. She pushed herself from the chair and started for the door. She moved a little like she was drunk, hands in her back pockets again, singing along with the Mumford & Sons song coming from the ceiling. Landon took note of the lyrics. He wondered how many different darkened lands Joy herself had wandered round.

The other coffee-goers watched her as she passed. Men and women alike. It was impossible not to notice her. It was impossible not to be impressed. She was beautiful and confident and strange.

Landon followed a few steps behind. He enjoyed watching her go. He noticed a man with a ponytail, scruffy beard, neck tattoo, leather bracelets. The man lowered his sunglasses and raised his brow as Joy walked past him.

"She has a good voice," Landon said. "Doesn't she."

He continued to follow Joy out of the shop. To anyone watching, it might not look like they were leaving together, but that's what they were doing. He enjoyed knowing they were leaving together. Landon thought about the phrase *leaving together*. There was a certainty to it, which gave him comfort.

Joy, in her journal

He lives in a house. He has a garden. He
picked a daisy from his garden and gave it to me.
I held the stem with two hands and set my nose to
the petals. I put the daisy in my hair and we went
inside and he made popcorn in an old-fashioned
popper. He melted butter on the stove. He played
Johnny Cash on an old record player and we
drank root beer in glass bottles with paper straws.
We sat on his couch and watched "Time Enough
At Last." From his boxed set. (*I knew it!*) I liked
how the actors spoke. Like they weren't trying to
be exactly real.

When I said I should go he didn't ask why
and he called me a cab. We sat on the front step
and a rabbit came onto his lawn and ate the white
clover. We watched it pluck and chew stem after
stem after stem. When the rabbit had had its fill,
it seemed to look at us for a moment, and then
it hopped away. It made me think of *Watership
Down*. When the cab came I kissed him (Landon,
not the rabbit, not the cabbie), and on the ride
back to my building I decided to make this blue-
eyed stranger mine.

I could be wrong, but I get the feeling he
would do anything for me.

Landon, not quite to himself

I've decided.

You don't know the first thing about living in the country.

What's to know? I've stayed here long enough.

This house was important to them. Your parents.

What's that thing Joy said before she left?

One cloud feels lonely.

That's what I feel like now. In this house. One cloud.

THREE IS A GOOD NUMBER

—◆◆◆—

For the third day in a row Joy and Landon entered The Pinecone Café together. To his relief, the chairs by the fireplace were empty. Before going to the counter he took off his jacket and hung it neatly over the back of the chair he considered his. Joy watched him. The song in the background finished and a new one began. Feist started counting. Joy sang along. I will, Landon thought. I will always tell you that I love you more.

This place had become their place.

He looked at her.

She linked her arm with his and they approached the counter. In the moment, she reminded him of Dorothy. He could see himself as the Tin Man, but never the Lion or the Scarecrow.

"So," he said. "We're off to see the wizard."

Joy gasped. "That's exactly what I was thinking."

—◆—

At the counter, the barista greeted them. "Look at you two. Third day in a row. You're becoming family."

Landon was sure he knew what the barista meant but he let himself hear the sentence another way and he liked in his head how the other way sounded.

Again, the barista reminded Joy of Victoria, from Victoria. She thought of the city and the woman in the city whose name was the same as the city. The city and the woman she had loved. Victoria, she thought. Victoria. The sea salt smell of the island air. From their balcony. Quiet and leaning against each other in the oversized wicker wingback, her own fingertips playing against Victoria's fingertips, like two spiders discovering love.

"Does that mean we'll be sisters?" Joy said.

The barista smiled. "Sisters."

Joy imagined painting the barista. A close-up portrait of her eyes and the jagged green bangs pasted to her forehead. The glitter of the ring in her nose. *Sisters.*

"Well, sister. We should introduce ourselves. I'm Joy and this is Landon."

"Nice to meet you. I'm Ghazal. Like the poem."

"Well, Ghazal-like-the-poem. I like your nose ring. I like that it's a skull."

"Most people think I'm into metal and bikers, but it's supposed to be for Hamlet."

Joy touched her mouth, pulsed her eyes. "That's the first thing I thought of."

"Really."

"A fellow of—"

"—*Infinite Jest.* Ohmygod, I love that book."

Landon had no idea what these two women were talking about but he watched them, back and forth, like a tennis match. He looked at Ghazal and said he did not know what he felt like today. Ghazal laughed and so did Joy.

The bell dinged and a group of twenty-somethings fell through the door like they were in a commercial. Landon turned, took note of them. Ghazal looked, too. Joy did not. Joy reached into the bowl on the counter and took one of the decorative pinecones from it. She put the pinecone in her pocket.

Ghazal looked at Joy.

Joy wondered if Ghazal had seen what she had done.

"You know what you should try?" Ghazal said. "The maple cappuccino." She leaned over the counter and whispered. "It's better than sex."

Landon put a fist to his mouth and cleared his throat. "Maple, you say."

Joy and Ghazal looked at each other and laughed again. They were sisters. They couldn't help themselves.

WELL

❖❖❖

Landon lay on the bed and watched the ceiling fan spin slowly around.

Things were going well.

Better than well.

Exceedingly well.

The word *well* rose to the clean white page in his mind. He thought of an old-fashioned stone well, one with a wooden arch above it and a wooden bucket attached by a length of rope, a handle you turned one way to lower the bucket down in and the opposite to draw it back to the surface, wet from the plunge, awash with the clean cold water collected within it.

He thought of the house in the country. The listing mentioned a stone well. He thought he might like to collect water in the mornings from such a well and drink the water standing there from a tin cup.

Landon sat up in the bed and looked at Joy. She was sleeping, one hand curled under her chin, the other buried beneath a pillow. He wanted to touch her but his hands were cold. He blew on them and pulled the blanket over her. She stirred. She settled. He watched her. She looked peaceful. She looked like she had always been there. She looked like a figure in a dream. She looked like the heroine in a fairy tale.

◆

Landon dressed and left the room and went to the closet in the front hall where he had stowed the gift he had made. He took the gift from the closet shelf and went to the kitchen where he set the gift on the table. He uncorked the bottle of Valpolicella he had purchased. The woman at the store seemed to know about wines and had recommended it. The woman at the store had told him about the importance of letting wine breathe. The man who wore sweaters said something similar: a simple but effective method to achieve or maintain a level calmness was to take a single deep breath, hold it, and then exhale.

Landon went to the record player and switched it on. He made sure the volume was low so as not to disturb Joy. He knew exactly where to set the needle. He had been listening to "Run On for a Long Time" over and over and over again. He liked the image of God as a lumberjack, cutting someone down like a tree.

◆

Joy padded into the kitchen. Landon was sitting at the table. She placed a hand on his shoulder. A tea candle was burning in a votive holder. A lighter lay beside it. The wine bottle and two glasses stood like silent attendants near the gift.

Joy was wearing a pair of Landon's work socks and one of his T-shirts, which came down to the middle of her thighs. She put a fist to her mouth and yawned. She sat in his lap. She tucked her hair. "What's all this?"

He liked that she sat in his lap. "I got you something."

She put an arm around his neck and kissed him, a hand on his chest. "You *got* me something?"

"Well—to be accurate—I made it."

He reached for the gift on the table, careful not to bump the candle, and pulled it closer. She took it in her hands and shook it. The pinecones rattled. She smelled the wrapping paper. It was a strange thing to do, Landon thought, but if anyone ever gave him a gift he was sure he would do the same.

"What is it?"

"Go ahead. Open it."

Joy tore into the paper and flipped the shoebox lid. She gasped a little and touched her mouth. Carefully, she removed the canoe and held it in her hands.

"I love it." She looked in Landon's eyes like she had lost something there.

She set the canoe on the table, stood, and went to Landon's room without a word. She returned with the pinecone she had taken from the café. She held out her hand and gestured for him to take it, and so he did.

She sat in his lap again.

He brought the pinecone to his nose and smelled it.

She smiled and reached for the wine and poured for them both. Landon set the pinecone on the table. They clinked glasses.

"My well runneth over."

"Cup," she said and touched his nose.

She kissed him again and he liked that he could taste the wine on her lips.

PAGES

—◆◆◆—

Joy spent the night and in the morning, over coffee, Landon told her there was something he wanted to show her.

She grinned. "I'm not going in the basement."

"It's not in the basement. It's at the library. Online."

She looked around the kitchen. She pictured the bedroom and the living room in her mind. She looked at him.

"You don't have a computer."

"No. I don't."

"You're an actual Luddite."

"I have a record player."

"Hah. See?" She pointed at him. "You are funny."

"Anyway. Can I show you?"

She put her cup down and looked at him. She folded her hands in her lap. "Yes. You can show me."

—◆—

The local branch was down the street. It was small for a library and looked like a house. Inside, it smelled of wood and the mustiness of old pages. The plank floor creaked when you walked on it. There were three computers in the middle of the main floor and aisles of books around the perimeter. When they walked in, two of the computers were occupied.

"We'll wait."

Joy looked at Landon. She didn't have to ask why.

Taking him by the arm, she leaned in and whispered, "This is my chance."

She moved through the place like it was her own home and Landon followed. Down one aisle she ran a finger across the spines. When she found the book she was looking for she slid it free and took Landon to a corner with two leather chairs and a window.

"Here," she said. "This is perfect."

They sat. Joy looked out the window. In the brightness a little girl spun a hula-hoop on her hips. The hula-hoop went round and round and round. The little girl's mother, nearby, was busy with her phone. Clouds gathered, which weakened the sun.

"I want to read this to you."

"Out loud?"

"Yes."

"But we're in a library."

Joy smiled. "Exactly. Now listen."

She began to read: "'The train went on up the track out of sight, around one of the hills of burnt timber…'"

Landon could see the train. He could smell the burnt timber.

It took Joy twenty minutes to read the story. Landon listened to every word. He could see everything she said and some of it he felt.

She closed the book. "So. What did you think?"

Landon thought about the question. He thought about it and then he answered.

"I like that there was a river. I like that the character could see the fish in it. When you read the line, *The earth felt good against his back*, I could feel it. I could feel the earth against my own back."

Joy smiled and pressed the closed book between her hands. "It's amazing, isn't it? How something that never actually happened can feel like it did."

Listening to Joy read reminded Landon of the time the man who wore sweaters had done the same, though the feelings that accompanied each experience were quite different. The man had read the opening of a novel called *A Death in the Family*. Landon took and read the book on the man's suggestion, but it did not help the way the man said it would. Landon had not read a novel since.

They'd been on their way to the man's office, he and his parents, when the accident happened. Landon thought about the phrase *accident happened*. *Happened* wasn't the word. *Happened* speaks of chance, of coming upon, of something taking place without intention—all of which are true to the accident, of course, but the word itself was forgettable. Whatever the accident was, it was not forgettable. It was the opposite of forgettable. Certain details were permanent. The sun glinting off the chrome fender of the vehicle in front of them. The oncoming van, its veering. The suddenness of the impact. How slow and fast and loud and silent it all was. The simultaneous feeling of knowing exactly where he was and not knowing at all. The incongruousness of being thrown forward while being held in place. The absolute stillness in the aftermath. The car radio flashing its time inches from his face in the backseat. The scented pinecone his mother had made and hung from the rearview by a length of twine somehow now in his lap. The feeling of it and always the smell. Then the angry, desperate sound of the car roof being attacked. The sudden ragged hole, the metal clawed and ripped away. The sky and the air and the blueness and the light. The hands reaching down like some kind of god to pull him free.

"Sometimes," he said, "the opposite is true. When something has actually happened, it can feel like it never did."

Joy looked at him. She stood and peeked around the corner. The computers were free.

"Your turn."

"My turn."

Landon thought she wanted him to read.

"I showed you. Now you show me."

She reached for his hand and pulled him out of the chair. He liked that she seemed always to know what she was doing. He liked how in control she was and he wondered how such control was even possible.

—◆—

They sat at the computers and Landon pulled up the listing:
"The Hart Farm"
R.R.#5, Lowbone.
50 acres.
1500 sq. ft. farmhouse. Partial basement, unfinished. Good for storage.
Hay and cattle barn. In good condition. Potential shop.
100 ft. of riverfront.
Original stone well. Good working condition.
5 acres of cedar woods.
15-minute walk to town. 50-minute drive to the city.
Reduced price.

Landon liked all of the 5s. He liked all of the 0s. He liked all of the goods.

"This is it." He clicked the mouse. "This is what I wanted to show you."

Joy looked at the old farmhouse on the screen. She clicked through the pictures. Everything looked old: the wooden floors, the windows, the woodstove, the well. There was a night shot of the house with the woods in the background that reminded her of Gainsborough's *Wooded Moonlight Landscape*.

"It's been on and off the market for years," Landon said. "The price keeps dropping. For some reason no one ever buys it."

Joy continued to click. "Bodies in the basement again."

"I'd like to go see it."

Hand still on the mouse, she looked at him. "What's stopping you?"

He shrugged. "I'm worried, I suppose."

"About what?"

"That it might not be what I want it to be."

She turned in her chair so that her knees touched his. She took one of his hands and pressed it between hers. "Nothing ever is."

He looked at his wrist where his hand seemed to disappear, her hands like the cover of a book, his like the pages within. "I'd like you to come with me."

Her shoulders fell. She tilted her head. "I'd love to."

Joy, in her journal

One day I was waiting for a bus in Dublin. A man
cleared his throat and asked me for a light. I looked
up. He was beautiful. I lit his cigarette. He inhaled
and exhaled and said thank you. He smiled. "Those
things are addictive." He indicated the cellphone
in my hand. "They'll kill you." I lit a cigarette of
my own. "I know. I've been meaning to quit." On a
whim I flipped the cellphone into the nearby trash
can. His eyes widened and he laughed. He took out
his own cellphone, looked at it for a moment, and
threw it in the trash with mine. The phones made
love in the dark on the heap and we did the same
on the floor of the empty room he was squatting
in. After, he lit a cigarette and told me his name.
Sly. Made up for sure, but what the hell, let him be
who he wants. Sly asked if I'd ever opened my eyes
in one particular place and then closed them that
same day in another particular place entirely. "Like
where?" I asked. "Like here," he said, "and then
Johannesburg." Lying there with this stranger, the
sun driving hard through the window, I lied and
said, "No. But I'd like to." We bought two tickets
and flew to South Africa. I began to paint. I got
good at it. I kept the ticket stub from the Mumford
& Sons concert. On the back Sly wrote, *You are joy*.
I took the pen and wrote, *You are sly*. Whenever I
open my music box and sift through the memories,
I flip the ticket in my hands and snicker at the truth
speaking to me from another time.

Before Sly in Johannesburg there was Barry in
Dublin, a man twice my age. Barry was hung but
Barry was boring and so Barry lasted less than a
month. I kept a Guinness coaster from the night
we met. I liked the gold harp and the font. Before
Barry, sad Paul in São Paulo. I was through with

sad Paul in a fortnight. Sad Paul used words like
fortnight hoping people would take him seriously.
I took sad Paul's mood ring, stuck permanently
on purple as it was. Before Paul, I bathed on the
beaches in Barcelona, alone. I found a perfect
pink shell on one of the beaches and when I
listen to it now there is only quiet. There was no
quiet with Stadtler and Silke in Berlin. I pulled
Silke's silk scarf from her neck the night we met
and slipped it into my pocket. When I run the
sheerness of it over my face I can still smell her
skin. I left Berlin for Marseille where I answered
an ad for an au pair. Within a minute of meeting
Sophie and Michel they both said they had a good
feeling about me. I had a good feeling about them,
too. I told them I always trusted good feelings. We
shared a lot of good feelings, separately together,
until one found out about the other. Later I found
a tiny doll's glass slipper in my coat pocket. It was
five-year-old Rebecca's. She was always playing
Cinderella. She was always looking for somewhere
to hide the glass slipper.

From Victoria I took only feelings.

Now here. Now Landon.

What to say about him?

He's not sly, or anywhere near it. He's my age,
or close enough. He's not sad but he is quiet. No
one else in his life will find out about us. There is
no one else in his life. (Which is maybe what I've
been looking for. Someone fundamentally alone.
Because that's what I am. What I have been. So
often and for so long. Even when I'm not. Even
when I wasn't.) And even though he does not
have a lip ring or a nose ring or any other kind of
ring, his lips are soft and his body is not and I do
enjoy kissing them both.

Landon, not quite to himself

She seemed taken with the house in the country.

She did.

She seems taken with me.

Despite all odds.

I worry.

About what?

What will happen.

Deep breaths.

Yes.

Listen. There's no point in worrying. You can't know what will happen until it does.

THE HART FARM

—◆◆◆—

Landon and Joy drove the hour north from the city to Lowbone and met Marty Pine as planned at the top of the long driveway near the farmhouse porch. Marty was leaning against his truck, arms folded. He looked the part: balding but doing his best to conceal it, a little paunchy, short sleeve shirt and tie, pants that were not quite long enough, and shoes that looked like they'd been prescribed by a doctor. Joy took note as she exited their car: *Willy Loman, a Study*. Landon joined her. Marty approached them. Everyone smiled. Handshakes ensued.

Landon looked around. "We've been watching this place. For a while."

Joy noted the use of *we*. Being here, with her, meant a lot to him.

Landon looked at Marty. "We're excited to be here."

"Excited's a good thing," Marty said. "Allow me to show you around."

There was a plaque near the steps that named the place. It looked like an award. Landon placed an open hand on the plaque's surface. It was smooth and cold and the words were etched into it. He removed his hand and looked at the palm, like he expected an imprint of the words to be there.

"Built in 1887," Marty said, "by one Robert Hart. He and his wife passed away in 1931. Their son, Robert Jr., had the place until 1965 with his wife, until they both passed, and then their son, the last Robert Hart, lived here until 1999 with his wife,

Molly. And now—" He spread his arms wide. "Here we are. Twenty years later and not a soul has lived in the house since."

Joy tucked her hair. "Don't you think that's strange?"

Marty folded his arms.

Joy looked up to the second-floor window. "Maybe it's haunted."

Marty watched her walk along the edge of the wild flower garden that spanned the length of the porch. She bent down and plucked a daisy. She smelled the flower and spoke to it.

"We love a good ghost story." She put the flower in her hair and stepped to Landon. She bumped him with her hip. "Don't we."

Marty didn't know what to say.

Landon was looking at the front door. He sensed a presence. In his mind he opened the door and looked beyond the threshold. Within the house, he could see himself and Joy at the table. Having coffee. The coffee was strong and dark and good. He could see his mother's record player. The arm was down and a record was spinning. He could hear the music. Like the singer was speaking directly to him. Telling him to close his eyes and have no fear. The monster was gone. The monster was on the run.

Joy tapped Landon on the shoulder.

He looked at her. "Forgive me. I was in my head."

Joy used her invisible wand. "Landon's big on forgiveness. Landon thinks a lot."

Marty was at a bit of a loss. This wasn't the kind of small talk he was used to. He dug in his pocket for the keys, then smiled and ascended the steps.

Joy and Landon followed. Joy went first. She reached back for Landon's hand. He looked at the hand. *Come on, Landon,* said a voice in his head. *What are you waiting for?*

◆

Marty opened the door, which creaked, and they entered the house. The first room was the kitchen. There was a bench built into the wall by the door. There were hooks by the door for coats and hats. Landon sat on the bench and gripped the edge. He looked around.

Joy stepped to the middle of the kitchen and turned a full circle on her heel. The curtains on the windows looked new, as did the appliances. She noticed the two place settings on the table and a vase with fresh flowers and two chairs set at a welcoming angle.

"It doesn't feel like it's been empty for twenty years."

"We try to keep it up to date. Never know when good folk like yourselves will come along."

"Good folk. Like us."

She smiled and walked around the kitchen, trailing her fingers over the surfaces. "I don't know about Landon, but I don't think I've ever been called good in my life.

She opened a cupboard and looked inside.

Marty touched a finger to his lips. "Can I get you something?"

Joy turned to him and shook her head.

Marty folded his arms high on his chest and cocked his head. "What is it you folks do? There's only so much a place like Lowbone can offer in the way of work, and I'm always curious what those who come here come here doing."

Landon was still sitting on the bench. He realized he did not know what Joy did in the way that Marty was asking.

"Landon's a woodworker." Joy lay a hand on her chest. "And I paint."

"Like pictures?"

She tilted her head a little at Marty. "Yes. Like pictures."

Landon thought of the painting of the barn in the coffee shop, how Joy had said that anyone could paint, that it couldn't be that hard, and now he couldn't help but wonder how much of what she said she did not really mean.

Marty put his hands together. "Well. I think this is the perfect spot for—what do you call it—inspiration."

Joy looked at him. She went to the closet near the front door and opened it. Inside, two metal hangers jangled when she touched them. An old straw hat sat on the shelf which she took and put on.

"It's such a beautiful hat," she said. "I will have a hat for every day of the week and an extra one just in case." She sounded like she might cry. "They will all be such beautiful hats."

Joy took the hat from her head and sat in Landon's lap. She put the hat on his head. She touched his nose and kissed him. "Do you know where that's from?"

He told her he did not.

"*The Great Gatsby*. It's a novel. About secrecy and love."

Marty was watching them. "Novels, eh? I like old westerns myself. Louis L'Amour. Zane Grey. That sort of thing." He set a hand like a wall to the side of his mouth, as though he meant to whisper a secret. "Plenty of cozy nooks in this old house to curl up in and read."

Joy pulsed her eyes at him. "Okay. Marty. Let's go take a look at those nooks."

After the nooks, they returned to the porch. A spring breeze rose and blew a cluster of leaves past the rail.

Marty loosened his tie and looked at his watch. "I don't know about you folks, but I could eat the hind end of a hog. If you're not in too much a hurry, what do you say we meet back here after lunch. You can have a look around town. Get a feel for it. Check out the shops. Have a bite to eat yourselves. Nice place on the main street called The Heather. Can't miss it."

"The shops," Joy said. "I can't say I expected shops."

"You know, standard little places. The hardware. The feed store. The apothecary. The grocer. The Arms & Gallery. There's a bookstore I'm sure you'll like. Called 'Turn the Page'. Rose'll be there. Nice lady. Sure knows her books."

"Turn the Page," Joy said and looked at Landon. "How fitting."

"Anyway, if you stop at The Heather for lunch you can't go wrong with the soup. It's damned good. Tell Esther I sent you. She'll take care of you."

"Esther. Okay. And the soup." Joy looked at Landon. He nodded. She looked at Marty. "We think that sounds like a wonderful idea. Marty."

"Good."

"Good?"

"Good."

"Good."

"What's say we meet back here for two, then."

Landon looked at his father's watch.

"Two it is," Joy said.

Marty went to his truck, climbed in, and drove away.

Landon and Joy followed.

A scarf of dust in their wake.

THE HEATHER

—◆◆◆—

The door dinged as Landon and Joy entered and the floors creaked beneath them. The Heather was quiet save the distant music coming from beyond the swing-door where the kitchen was. Only one customer sat at the counter. All the tables were empty.

Joy leaned in and whispered to Landon. "I think you should try to be a little friendlier."

He furrowed his brow.

"You don't say very much."

"I said we were excited to be here."

"Yes."

"I am, you know. Excited."

"You just need to—relax a little."

Landon breathed in and held it. He exhaled. He took a committed step towards the counter. The man sitting there on a stool turned to take in Lowbone's most recent visitors.

Landon unzipped his jacket and nodded once. "Fine spring day."

The man at the counter scratched the black-and-grey stubble on his chin. He was thick everywhere: wrists, neck, waistline. He wore a cable-knit sweater, like a fisherman. "Do I know you?" He folded his arms over his chest. "I think I'd remember a city boy like you."

Landon looked confused. Although he'd lived in the city his whole life he did not consider himself a city boy, an expression that he understood as having something to do with sophistication. Landon wore jeans and plain shirts every day. He wore the same jacket in the spring and the fall. His one winter coat was ten years old and still in fine condition. He did not like the noise or the bustle of the city streets. He never went out at night. He bought groceries once a week at a store that used paper bags. He drove a twenty-year-old sedan that he had inherited from his mother and father and he did all the maintenance on it himself. He worked with his hands. He had, in every way he could while still living there, disconnected from the city. He wanted, and had wanted for a long time, to make The Hart Farm his home, to make Lowbone the place where he lived. He wondered how all of this wasn't obvious. At the very least he wondered how a stranger at a single pass could so poorly misinterpret who he was.

"No. You don't know me. But—"

"But nothing," the man said. "I don't see things ending well for you here."

Landon pocketed his hands and stared at the grain in the plank floor. Someone had gone to great pains to maintain the finish. He looked up and shook his head once.

The man at the counter turned on his stool and set his back to Landon.

Joy went to him and whispered. "That went well."

She ushered him to a table by a window.

Clouds moved in and it started to rain.

A woman appeared through the swing door behind the counter and the volume of the music rose for a moment. The song: "I'm So Lonesome I Could Cry."

She approached Joy and Landon at their table. The woman's mole-brown hair was tied back in a ponytail. Loose strands hung by her face. Her features, Joy thought, were featureless. Aside from the cursively stitched name above the left shirt pocket where "Esther" kept a small ringed notepad, there was no immediate way to identify who this woman was, forgettable in every way but her plainness.

"What'll youse have?" Esther said, pen at the ready.

Joy made eye contact. "Marty Pine told us the soup was to die for."

"I wouldn't die for no soup, but yeah, it ain't bad."

Joy closed the menu and pressed it between her hands. "I'll have whatever the soup of the day is. And coffee. Black."

Esther jotted the order in her pad and looked at Landon.

Sensing her eyes on him he turned from the window and looked at her. He'd been watching the rain. "I'd just like to say, I meant no offence to that man. I meant only to make his acquaintance."

"Who, Bill? He's harmless." She leaned forward a little. "Unless he really don't like you."

Landon couldn't tell if Esther was joking. He picked up the menu but did not open it. Landon never opened a menu. Whenever he ate out, which wasn't often, he always ordered the special. It was easier and he figured if it was the special it must be fresh and it must be good. He set the menu down. "I'll have the special," he said. "And an espresso."

Esther stopped writing. She looked at him over the notepad.

"He means coffee," Joy said. "He'll have the special and a coffee. Black."

Esther nodded, collected the menus, and left.

Landon looked out the rain-streaked window. Joy reached across the table and touched his arm.

"Let's play a game."

This was Bill. He was staring across the counter, his back to Joy and Landon, but he spoke in a voice loud enough for them to hear.

"Here's how it works. I ask you a question, you tell me the answer." He drew on his cigarette and drank from his mug.

Landon closed his eyes.

Joy saw how stuck Landon was. She swivelled in her seat and smiled at Bill even though he could not see her because he was still facing away. She made her voice light. "What do you want to know?"

"I want to know how it is you ended up here."

"Just passing through."

"No one passes through Lowbone."

What Bill said sounded like a fact, but it also sounded like a threat.

Joy turned to Landon. She squeezed his arm. He opened his eyes and stared out the window. The street was empty and the rain was coming down.

"Try again," Bill said.

Joy tucked her hair. "We're here to look at The Hart Farm."

Bill turned on his stool to face Joy. She noticed the stillness of his left eye. Even with the distance between them she could see the three scars that began above his brow and continued downward. Like he'd been clawed. "The Hart Farm's no place for a peach like you."

Joy felt something falter inside her. Her shoulders fell.

Bill turned on his stool, setting his back to Lowbone's most recent visitors again. He finished what was in his mug and rubbed his cigarette out in the tray. He stood and nodded to Esther. The door dinged when he left.

Esther brought Joy and Landon their orders. After a while Landon stopped staring out the window. He pulled the toothpicks from his sandwich and ate. He drank his coffee.

Joy spooned her soup. She thought about the words Marty Pine had used to describe it. It felt like the words were hanging in the air.

Damned.

Good.

TURN THE PAGE

◆◆◆

Joy pulled the door open, which set off a dinging, like in The Heather, and when she stepped inside, the wooden floors creaked even more noticeably than they had in the restaurant. Joy looked up and noted the verdigris-mottled copper bell the size of a fist and thought it looked a thousand years old. She would paint the bell and take up the whole canvas doing it: *For Thee.* Oversized, soft-looking, fabric-worn armchairs sat in a nook on one side of the door, angled so their occupants might look up from their books when they wanted and peer through the spider-cracked old window that looked onto the quiet Lowbone main street. A white cat slept on the wide white paint-flaking wooden sill. On the other side of the door was an exposed-brick wall. On the wall hung a window-sized painting of a wooded river. Standing on the shore and casting into the river was a man wearing a brimmed hat and a beard and an expression of solace and contemplation. Clandestinely perched in the trees above him, an owl peered down at the man. The moon, white like the owl, was a hook in the night sky above the woods and the light of the moon glinted off the rippled surface of the river. The artist's signature was small and indiscernible in the bottom right corner, an angled cursive thin white scrawl that bled into the year: '87.

Joy loved the smell of the old floors and the books and the hint of tea steeping. She loved how the floors creaked and moved beneath her like the floor itself was floating above an open space below. She wondered if there was a trap door somewhere, a set of stairs leading down, an ever-burning old-world torch nestled in a leather holder at the bottom of the stairs she might use to light the candle sconces hanging on the damp walls along the secret corridor. A chest tucked in a corner, full of books as old as the bell. Secrets of a lost time to unearth. Another world entire. Joy looked at the white cat sleeping on the sill. She saw the animal as an indifferent guard, unconcerned by the potential threat Joy posed to the merchandise that he, the cat, was sentry to. Joy wrinkled her nose at the cat and christened him Cerberus. She thought she might be able to fall asleep herself in one of the old chairs by the window. The chairs looked like tired, corpulent old men. Turning on a heel, she stepped to the other side of the door and lay a hand on the brick wall. She glanced over her shoulder and wondered how difficult it might be to steal the painting.

While Joy pondered, Landon stood in one spot and took his own notes. He appreciated the floor-to-ceiling shelves built into the walls that spanned the perimeter of the shop. They were thick and heavy and scarred and old. The books themselves were all erect and organized and flush, one with the next, establishing a perfectly uniform front. They seemed, to him, to be standing at attention, in ready opposition to those who might mean to peruse them. Anyone who liberated a volume but did not purchase it would feel compelled to return it to its exact position. Landon loved how strong and permanent the shelves looked. He loved the order.

Through a beaded curtain at the back of the store came a slight woman with an upright walk and a pixie cut of silver hair. Horn-rimmed silver glasses framed her bright grey eyes. There was an age in her face she was proud of and a look that spoke of a wit she kept sharp and at the ready. She wore a black woollen argyle skirt, pinned at the side with a silver brooch, and a bone-white ruffle-necked sweater. Stepping behind the island counter that sat in the middle of the store, she folded the tea towel she had been drying her hands with when she came through the curtain and set it on a shelf beneath the register.

She placed her hands on the counter, like a card dealer, and looked at Landon. Then she looked at Joy. "Most would guess you two are newly wed. My guess is newly met."

Joy folded her hands together and held them at her waist. She closed one eye and took one step forward, pointing both index fingers at the woman behind the counter. "I like you."

"Well, little siren. I'll wait to see what your taste is in books before uttering my reciprocal affection."

Joy clapped once and laughed. When Landon looked at the woman behind the counter he thought of his mother. They could have been sisters. They shared a slightness and a style, and when his mother was happy, she had had a similar way about her.

"You have a beautiful store. It feels like everything has been in place for a thousand years and will remain so for a thousand more. There is order and care."

The woman looked at Joy. "I like the way he speaks."

Joy bit her pinky finger. She took the finger from her mouth and stepped to the counter. She picked up a book and flipped through it. She set the book down and looked at the woman. "I don't think you're from here."

"How astute. What gave it away?"

Joy squared her shoulders and offered a formal hand across the counter. The woman shook hands with Joy and Joy took note of the ruby ring on the woman's middle finger. She brought the woman's hand closer, like she was about to kiss it.

"I like your ring."

"So do I. It has powers."

Joy looked up. The woman was grinning. One of her eyebrows, a high arch.

"I suppose we should do names. I'm Rose."

"Rose. How perfect. I'm Joy."

"Yes. Well. As perfect names go."

Landon watched these two women. They turned to him. He set a fist to his mouth and made a little noise in his throat. "My name is Landon. It's nice meet you."

"Yes," she said. "It is. Nice to meet you. Both." She placed her hands flat on the counter again. "You're planning to move here. Together. My guess is The Hart Farm."

Landon and Joy looked at one another, then at Rose.

"There are things you should know. Before you do."

Roused, the cat yawned. He pushed himself to his paws. Landon and Joy followed Rose's eyes and they all watched the cat arch his back, stretch, and drop to the floor. He moved, unhurried, to the back of the store and through the beaded curtain.

"Time for Dove's afternoon snack." She looked at them. "We are creatures of habit, each of us."

Rose stepped from behind the counter and disappeared behind the beaded curtain. Landon stood still. Joy went to a shelf and flipped through a few books.

Returning, Rose took her place behind the counter and looked at Joy. "Find anything?"

Joy closed the book she was holding and set it down. She approached the counter again and set her open hands upon it. Landon, wrists crossed behind his back, walked around the store. Joy leaned in asked Rose if she had a copy of *In Our Time.* "It's for Landon. He doesn't read much. But we're trying to fix that."

"Careful, little siren." Rose spoke so only Joy could hear. "Those we want most to mend are often broken in places we cannot see."

Joy watched Landon gather the books she had taken down. He scanned the shelves and returned the books to the exact places from which Joy had taken them.

Rose touched one of Joy's hands on the counter, smiled, and then walked from behind the counter to join Landon. She touched his shoulder. He looked at her hand on his shoulder and then he looked at her. She thanked him for his help and took a volume from a nearby shelf.

Landon checked his father's watch. "I think we should probably go. Mr. Pine will be waiting."

Rose handed Joy a paper bag. Joy peeked in and saw that it contained the book she had asked for. Joy lifted the bag to her face. She closed her eyes and smelled.

When she opened her eyes, Landon was beside her. He placed a hand to the small of her back. She looked at him. He smiled. She wanted to tell him something, but in the moment she could not think what.

Rose watched them. They looked at her.

"Nothing ever happens in Lowbone," she said, "but it always feels like something might."

THE WOODS

✦✦✦

J oy and Landon drove with the windows down. The air smelled
of earth and rain. Joy breathed in and closed her eyes. She
was smiling. When she opened her eyes she looked at Landon's
hands on the wheel. He was gripping the wheel rather tightly.

Marty was waiting for them again at the top of the
driveway, leaning against his truck. When they exited the car
Landon zipped his jacket and Joy hugged herself against the
breeze. Marty put a hand in the air and walked towards them.

"So. How'd you like the soup?"

Joy tucked her hair. "The soup. The soup was just as you
said."

Marty looked pleased.

Landon didn't speak.

Joy looked away from the house towards the woods. "So.
Marty. How far does this place go?"

Marty pointed where Joy was looking. "There's a trail
there. Takes you through to the other side where there's a river.
All part of the property."

Joy took Landon by the hand and started away. "Let's go
for walk. Through the woods."

✦

Marty got ahead of them. Landon and Joy followed. Near the beginning of the trail Joy noticed the remains of a small animal. A tuft of grey fur, a smattering of little bones. She stopped. Marty turned and noticed her stopping.

"Rabbit," he said. "Fox or something got it."

Joy thought of the rabbit eating clover on Landon's lawn in the city. "Are there wolves?"

Landon looked at her.

"Funny you should mention it. It's what usually brings outsiders to Lowbone. The wolf sanctuary, I mean. It's up the road and east of town a bit, maybe three miles. You'll hear them at night. Just like you imagine. One who runs it's something of a lone wolf himself. Should see it when he feeds them."

"You can watch?"

"Turns it into a bit of a show. Feeds them live prey. Chickens mostly. A deer when one gets hit by a car and doesn't quite die."

A pack of clouds crept in front of the sun. The shadows darkened. Landon felt a chill but he did not let himself shiver. Central to the sessions with the man who wore sweaters was a purposeful distancing from what had happened. Distancing, the man told him, establishes control. Landon had not yet decided if he would share what had happened with Joy. He had not yet decided if he could. He closed his eyes. He felt the chill again and the shadows and the coming of the wolf he was trying to keep at bay. As part of the exercise, he replaced the image of the wolf with the word *wolf* on the clean white page of his mind. He replaced the nominal meaning with the verbal. He felt a calmness. Distance, he thought. Control.

Joy touched his arm and Landon opened his eyes.

"You know," she said, "I think I love it here."

Landon looked down the trail. It seemed to go on forever. The air was cool and rich with cedar smells. The ground was soft. He could sleep on the ground. If he ever had to. He would feel his back on the ground, like the man in the story Joy had read him. He touched a nearby tree and assessed it. Everything about this place was exactly as he'd hoped. Exactly as he'd imagined. He was pleased by what Joy said. He loved it here, too. But the thought of it all actually happening—moving here, with Joy—worried him a little. Any sudden movement might undo it all.

THE BARN

––◆◆◆––

Marty grabbed the handle and dragged the old slatted door open, which took some effort. He stood back and hipped his hands.

"Here it is. Like the listing says, it's in good condition." He looked at Landon. "Handy as it sounds you are you should have her turned into a shop in no time."

Landon looked around. Light seeped in through the cracks and the holes in the barn board walls. A single bale of hay remained in the loft, the hay itself old and dust dry. The ladder leading to the loft looked solid. The smell of wood and hay and long-rotted manure hung faintly in the air. The stalls held no real evidence of the animals they once contained: hard-packed earth where hooves might have been, a bit of old straw strewn and worked into the corners, empty wooden troughs in each, rusted faucets that whined and produced no water when Landon tested them. An old wood-handled shovel leaned against the gate of one of the stalls and beside it a tin bucket, flipped over like a stool.

"What do you think?"

Landon nodded. He took the shovel and tested the heft of it. Stood the handle in the ground so the blade was level with his shoulder. He held the shovel there, one hand around the throat of it.

Joy thought he looked like one half of *American Gothic*. She moved in beside him, completing the image. She touched the small of his back. She turned to Marty.

A family of sparrows bantered in the rafters. One descended and perched on a post nearby. Joy watched it. She was certain the bird looked at her.

Marty folded his arms and cleared his throat. "There are a few things I have to tell you before we go any further. You remember I mentioned the last Robert Hart. And Molly."

Landon and Joy waited.

"See—the thing is—one day Molly up and disappeared."

Joy held up a hand. "Wait."

Marty looked at her.

This is where the transaction had ended for every other prospective buyer. Whatever it was Marty was about to say, it had been bad enough to shatter the glass that protected the portrait of what The Hart Farm might be. Joy did not want to shatter the glass.

She turned to Landon. "What if we said we didn't want to know?"

Marty, collecting on the good luck he felt he was due: "Well. That's up to you."

Landon nodded. Joy smiled and tucked her hair.

CITY TO COUNTRY

◆◆◆

Within two weeks Landon had listed and sold the house in the city, performed all the closing duties, packed everything he wanted to take with him, donated the rest, and organized the movers. In one afternoon, he had helped Joy clear out her apartment. She had one suitcase, a music box, four crates of books, three canvases, a jar full of brushes, and a few tubes of paint. From the balcony she also took the wrought iron table and chair that weren't hers. On the front of an envelope she sketched a woman with a suitcase walking towards the edge. She put her keys in the envelope and slipped the envelope through the slot by the front doors. Joy's envelope did not contain a rent cheque. She had not given notice. She never did.

Joy, in her journal

How much of what happens do we really control? How much of what happens happens *to* us and not *by* us? One afternoon I'm in the heart of the city in the heart of a store I could never afford to buy anything from when a stranger bumps into me. A strange stranger. A really strange stranger. We talk. We get coffee. We do it again the next day. We go back to his place and he makes popcorn and we drink root beer from glass bottles and he plays Johnny Cash on a record player he tells me he inherited from his mother. I don't ask about the inherited part and he doesn't say.

He gives me a canoe he carved himself. Carved! Himself!

He doesn't own a computer or a cellphone so we go to the library because he wants to show me something online. He pulls up a listing for a beautiful old house no one has lived in for twenty years in a small town an hour north of the city.

So we go.

It's everything the pictures made it out to be. The property goes on, it seems, forever. It has its own forest, its own river. Like something out of a myth. The house itself is like a painting.

We drive into town. We walk around. We have lunch. We visit the bookstore. We meet Rose. A rose of a Rose. I loved her instantly. In forty years I want to be her. She tells us there are things we should know about the farm before we buy it, but she doesn't tell us what. So we don't ask. Marty said one of the previous owners, Molly, just up and disappeared one day. He used

the word *up*. Which changes things. It's different
from disappeared by itself. Up and disappeared.
What does that mean? Was she kidnapped? Did
she vanish in the night? Did she wake up one
morning and look at her husband over coffee and
decide she had to go?

Marty was going to tell us. He was about to.
He said he *had* to tell us.

Then I blurted out, "*What if we said we didn't
want to know?*"

I looked at Landon. He nodded. Before I
knew it we were in town signing the papers.

I shouldn't have said anything. Of course
I want to know. How could I not? How could
anyone?

Landon, not quite to himself

Are you going to tell her what happened?

What if she'd rather not know?

Wouldn't you want to know, if something similar had happened to her?

I don't know.

You should tell her.

I will. Maybe I will.

Without mentioning it to Joy, Landon went to The Pinecone Café one more time before they left the city for good. Ghazal wasn't there. He didn't know the woman behind the counter, which made him feel relieved. He wouldn't have to make small talk and he wouldn't have to explain where Joy was. He wouldn't have to explain that they were leaving.

He walked up to the counter and ordered a small dark roast to go. The barista, the stranger, smiled and went about filling his order. The moment she turned away Landon drew a pinecone from his jacket pocket—the pinecone Joy had taken the last time they were here together—and placed it in the bowl on the counter. Amongst the others, it was noticeable in no particular way. He would be the only one for the rest of time who knew it was there.

He looked at the three stacks of business cards on the counter. One had Ghazal's name and her number. He took one of the cards for Joy.

The barista returned with Landon's coffee and handed it to him. He paid and dropped a few coins in the tip jar. He turned to leave but stopped himself.

"Thank you."

"You're welcome." She smiled. "See you again."

Landon nodded. He turned and walked towards this particular door for the last time.

He recognized the singer in the background. Something Ross. She was singing about how people make her nervous, that she misses everyone she's never met.

—◆—

Joy and Landon stood in the driveway and watched the movers load the last of their things into the van. One of the movers lifted and walked the ramp into the underbelly of the vehicle while the other mover jumped down from the cargo bay. When the ramp was secure, the second of the movers stepped on the

fender, reached up for the strap, and hauled the door down on
its rollers. The first mover swung the locking arm into place
and secured it.

Joy held onto Landon. "It's like all of our stuff just got
thrown in jail."

The movers climbed into the cab of the van and backed
onto the street.

Joy waved to them like they were family she hadn't seen
in a year and it would be just as long before she saw them again.
The driver smiled and raised a hand in return. Landon watched
them go.

Landon turned and walked towards the house. Joy went
with him. He stopped a few paces from the front step.

He took a breath and held it. She watched him.

"One last look around?"

"—."

Landon exhaled and went up the steps. Joy watched. He
took a small object from his jacket pocket and held it in the
cradle of his fingertips. It was the pinecone that had not fit in the
canoe. He bent down and buried the pinecone in the earth that
filled the planter his mother had always grown carnations in.
Maybe the next owners would do the same. Maybe they would
discover the pinecone and wonder. Maybe when the soil began
to warm in the sun and the pinecone opened and freed the seeds
one of the seeds would take root. Maybe a seedling would grow
like a finger from the earth. Maybe the next owners would plant
the seedling in the yard and their grandchildren would collect
the pinecones from the tree that eventually grew. Maybe the
pattern would go on forever.

Landon was thinking all of this as he brushed the dirt
from his hands on the front of his pants.

He turned and walked down the steps.

Arms still folded, Joy gestured with her head that they
should go. She did not ask him what he had done.

They looked at each other across the top of the car. They
climbed in and closed the doors. Landon started the vehicle.
They pulled on their seatbelts. Joy clicked the radio on. Landon

slid the car into gear and drove away. It was a choreography each seemed to intuit and neither felt the need to say a word.

UNPACKING

—◆◆◆—

That evening Landon and Joy stood on the porch of The Hart Farm and watched the movers drive away. A cloud of dust in their wake.

Joy put both hands to her mouth and laughed but not loudly.

Landon looked at her.

Still he had to tell himself not to stare.

What a strange conflation of feelings that comes with having wanted something for so long that suddenly comes to be.

He put an arm around her and she fell into him. He breathed in. He held her there.

—◆—

As the sun set, Joy and Landon popped the cork on a bottle of Valpolicella. They made love on the kitchen floor. They lay there, after, a single blanket between them and a pillow each, surrounded by boxes. Joy didn't like the phrase *make love*. It was a euphemism for people who close their eyes and shut the lights. Joy didn't close her eyes. The singer they were listening to told them to keep a light on and so they did. They drank more wine. They made more love. Joy fell asleep and Landon watched her for a while. Eventually he fell asleep, too, and they looked like victims lying there.

At two in the morning Landon woke, chilled by the night. At some point Joy had hijacked the blanket and was now wrapped fully within it, deep into whatever dream she was dreaming. Landon went to the porch, careful not to let the door snap shut, and clutched the rail. He looked out into the darkness and listened. Frogs croaked. Crickets chirped. Beyond the woods, somewhere on the river, a loon called. A beaver slapped its tail against the water. Like a single and lingering round fired from a gun.

—◆—

They woke late the next morning. Landon found the coffee maker and brewed a pot. Joy flipped through a crate of albums and selected Joni Mitchell's *Blue*. She held the album up and said Landon's name. He turned and when he saw the singer on the blue cover—eyes closed, sad-looking, contemplative—he smiled and nodded. It had been one of his mother's favourites. It was one of Joy's favourites, too. "River" was near the end of the album and Joy tried to get as close to it as she could with the needle. Landon found a box labelled "Dishes" and he pulled out two cups. He poured the coffee and they sat together with their backs against a wall in the kitchen. When the song ended they listened to "Case of You." Landon pushed himself from the floor and went to the record player and played the song again. He would do so one more time. Joy got up to refill her coffee and held the pot in the air. Landon said he was fine and rested his head against the wall behind him. He closed his eyes. He thought he might be happy but he wondered if that was the word.

Joy sat down beside him and rested her head on his shoulder. "Let's go see what we can find." Landon kept his eyes closed. Joy sang the chorus of "River." When she finished he opened his eyes and told her she didn't have to wish. There was a river on the other side of the woods. She could skate away on it in the winter whenever she wanted. In the spring and fall she could paddle away. In the summer she could swim. Whatever she wanted. She could do whatever she wanted to do. He didn't have to tell her this, of course. Joy did not need to be told about her freedom. She had, for a long time, practised it freely. But he felt good telling her. And she felt good hearing him tell her.

Joy stood and reached for Landon's hand. Together they went to the woods.

—◆—

As Joy and Landon emerged they saw a great blue heron bat its wide wings and lift from the far shore of the river. The way it moved through the air reminded Joy of what she had seen of dragons. She told Landon and he knew exactly what she meant. They stood on the dock and watched the river's slow current. The spring breeze rippled the surface. Landon pocketed his hands. Joy slipped a hand between one of Landon's arms and his body and tucked her other hand in her own pocket.

"We're like two links in a chain. A ghost's chain you can't see the beginning or the end of."

Landon nodded, although this time he knew only part of what she meant.

Lily pads curled on the surface nearby. They looked, he said, like little hands, beckoning.

Joy bit her bottom lip. "That's perfect. Do the weeds. There, under the water."

Landon thought for a moment. The weeds looked, he told her, like someone's long hair, blowing in a liquid wind.

—◆—

Landon and Joy took their time unpacking. In a little more than a week they were settled. Joy didn't like the word *settled* but settled is what they were. Like sediment resting in layers at the bottom of a lake. The eventual stillness of a freshly cleaned blanket snapped above a bed like a matador's cape. A sunflower's head hanging in the evening as the air cools and the sun winks goodnight.

Joy often noted thoughts like these in her journal. She noted what Landon had said about the lily pads and the underwater weeds. Sometimes she used what she wrote to inspire a painting. She had been writing in this particular journal for a decade. Flipping through it now, she saw the last ten years of her life in words. She was near the end. Soon she would need a new set of pages.

◆

Joy was on the bed, writing, when Landon came in.

"There you are."

She closed the journal. "Here I am."

"I cut some wood. I cleaned the flue and started a fire."

"I can smell it," she said. "I can feel it."

He sat on the edge of the bed and put a hand on one of her bare feet. He looked out the window. "I'm so—"

"Pleased?"

He looked at her. "Pleased. Yes."

He saw the word on the clean white page in his mind and the ends of the word fell away.

Ease.

Joy took her wine from the bedside table and drank. "Me too."

And in the moment, she was.

◆

Landon spent two weeks turning one of the bedrooms into a studio. He removed the carpet and restored the wood beneath. Joy said she liked the "scars" the floor had. He liked how she said it and told her he liked them, too. He doubled the size of the window. "An artist," she told him, "needs light." He painted the walls, on her request, a soft yellow. "Like the sun," she said, "pushing through the clouds." After he finished the studio, he turned to the barn. He tore out the stalls and blocked out a ceiling, keeping the loft as an attic. He poured a floor. Framed and insulated the walls. Cut and installed board and batten. Built shelves and three worktables. Organized his tools and material. Felled three cedars and had them milled into different thicknesses and widths.

The first thing he made was a frame for the old hammock he found in the basement. The basement itself made him think of the word *cellar*. It was dark and damp and cobwebby and the overhead bulbs were long blown. He used a flashlight to look around and happened upon a shelving unit against the back wall. The hammock was folded and placed neatly on the bottom shelf, set there at the close of some past summer. He thought Joy would like the hammock, so he took it from the basement and built the frame. He also found a length of milled hardwood that was the perfect size for a paddle. On the top shelf he found a few old tobacco tins filled with nails. In one of the tins he found a key attached to a length of leather string. He thought someone in the past must have worn the key like a necklace. He thought about draping it around his own neck. He liked the look of the key and the smell and the feel of the leather string. He took the key on the leather string and placed it in the drawer in the kitchen by the fridge.

When he was finished the frame he set up the hammock under the old maple tree in front of the house. Joy noticed him through the kitchen window. She was drinking a glass of wine. She joined him.

"I love it." She traced her fingers over the hammock's weave. "Imagine who has lain here."

Joy gave Landon her glass and he drank from it. She sat on the hammock's edge and used it like a swing. The frame creaked. She lay in it and crossed her arms over her chest.

"I feel like Ophelia."

The breeze lifted and the smell of lilacs came with it.

Landon set a hand on the frame he had built and watched Joy.

"Oh, we know what we are," she said. "But not what we may be."

THE WOLF DEN

—◆◆◆—

Harlon Glen let the screen door snap shut behind him and he pulled on his boots as he stepped onto the porch. He squatted beside the dog he called Girl. She was barking. He pet her and she settled.

"What is it, Girl?"

Harlon saw the truck he had traded in last fall idling in the distance where the Glen Road and the long driveway met. He saw two figures within the cab. He could not tell who they were.

Harlon scratched Girl behind the ears. "Now. Who do you suppose that is in our old truck?"

Not far from Harlon and his dog a fire burned in a barrel. Along with a heap of deadfall he had picked up around the yard and cut down to size to get the fire going were the remains of one stray cat and two rabbits: Girl's most recent victims. Deep within her DNA was the instinct to hunt and kill. Instead of eating what she killed, which was what her ancestors would have done, she deposited the bodies at the farmhouse door like a gift. Harlon always burned the bodies, which was better, he thought, than burying them or putting them out in the trash. If he buried them, the dog would only dig them up. If he put them out in the trash, the garbage collector might start to wonder and rumours might begin. It's how things had started going strange, so the story went, at The Hart Farm. Dead animals in the trash.

—◆—

Landon put the truck in park and looked up at the sign.

The Wolf Den.

Someone had taken great pains in the manufacture of this sign.

The letters were deeply and carefully carved and stained a darker brown than the rest of the wood. The whole thing was heavily lacquered.

Landon thought the sign looked impenetrable.

He sensed Joy's eyes on him. He liked the feeling that came with sensing Joy's eyes on him. For the moment he did not say a word. He continued to look at the sign, thinking about its seeming permanence.

—◆—

Harlon descended the porch steps, Girl beside him, and watched his old truck make its way up to the house like it was a long-lost pet finally finding its way home.

Landon stopped the truck a few paces from the porch and parked beside the truck that was already there. He and Joy exited the cab and walked towards Harlon who touched Girl's head with one hand and held the other up to his approaching visitors.

"Good day. Nice truck you got there."

Landon looked over his shoulder where he had parked the truck, then back at Harlon.

He didn't know what to say. He didn't want to be here, if he was being honest. Joy didn't know what being here would do to him or she wouldn't have asked him to come.

Joy looked at Harlon Glen and smiled. She tucked her hair. "The dealer said the previous owner had taken good care of it, and that he was a good man."

"Been called a lot of things." Harlon smiled with one side of his mouth. "Can't say good is one of them." He looked at Joy and stepped towards her, offering a hand.

Joy shook his hand and made note of what she saw: down-soft tawny hair the breeze liked to play with, sharp eyes deeply set and dark, a muscled body beneath the fitted shirt. He looked, she thought, like a Steinbeck character. When she painted him she would rest an axe on his shoulder. She would include the dog at his feet. *Man—in the Country.*

"Dealer's right, though. Took real good care of her."

Joy turned to Landon. "Didn't we find a pair of gloves in the glove compartment?" She looked at Harlon. "They must be yours."

"Keep them. Part of the deal."

"Don't be silly." Joy tucked her hair and turned for the truck.

Landon folded his arms and watched her go.

Harlon looked at the ground, then Landon.

The two men waited.

Joy returned and shrugged. "Couldn't see them."

"Not a worry."

"We'll be sure to get them to you, if we find them."

Landon didn't like this particular use of *we*.

Harlon nodded and looked at Joy for a moment longer than he'd intended. "You must be the folks who bought The Hart Farm."

Joy nodded.

"How're you settling in?"

Joy looked at Landon. "We love it."

Harlon watched her. "Good. That's good. It's good someone finally bought the place." He folded his arms. "So. What can I do for you?"

Joy slipped her hands in her back pockets and took a step towards him as though she meant to tell him a secret. She spoke quietly. "We were hoping to see the wolves."

"They'll be scarce today. Had the local Scouts here last night for a feeding."

Landon breathed in and held it. He exhaled. He felt something in the air. He turned and looked at the barrel where Harlon had a fire going. The fire was dying. The last wisps of smoke swirled from the top of the barrel, like the barrel itself was breathing.

"Got a group coming from the city the end of the week. You could join them if you want."

Joy bit her bottom lip, gripped Landon's arm with both hands. Her whole body tensed. "We'd love to."

Landon looked at her hands holding his arm. He looked at her face, her eyes.

Harlon showed his guests a hand and grinned. "See you Friday, then." The dog turned with him when he went.

Landon thought about what this man with the wolves had said. Two words stood out. *Scarce. Join.* The ends of the words fell off in Landon's mind and he pictured Harlon turning to him. *Scare. Joy.*

Landon wanted to go. He undid Joy's hands from his arm. He turned and started for the truck.

Joy stood there in the growing space between the two men, and then stepped in the direction of Harlon and his dog. "Wait," she said, but not urgently. "We didn't get your name."

Harlon turned and brushed the hair from his forehead. "Harlon. Harlon Glen."

"I'm Joy," she said, setting a hand to her throat. Blindly, she reached with her other hand for Landon who was now some distance from her. "And this is Landon." Landon heard his name. He turned and looked at the hand reaching for him. He could not not walk towards it.

"I know you said it's probably not worth it. But since we're here anyway, do you mind if we walk the trail?"

Harlon folded his arms. He looked at her. "Sure. Whatever pleases you."

"Thank you. Harlon."

Joy turned when Landon took her hand. She felt her heart thump a little quicker.

—◆—

They walked the trail through the woods and Joy remained unaware of Landon's unease. To Landon's relief, Harlon had been right. The wolves were somewhere deep within the woods, sleepy and sated from their meal the night before, uninterested and unmoved by the presence of these newcomers.

When Landon and Joy exited the trail they saw that Harlon's truck was gone. The screen door to the house was open and in the breeze the hinges creaked and the door itself snapped against the wood siding of the house.

Joy walked towards the porch and ascended the steps.

Landon watched her.

She took the door in her hand and clicked it closed. She peered through the window to the kitchen within. It looked almost identical to their own. There was even a record player set up in the corner.

She turned on a heel and descended the steps. Landon was picking something up from the ground. He put what he had picked up in his pocket. She reached for his hand as she approached him. He took it. They walked to the truck together, a breeze rising around them. Somewhere in the woods one of the wolves lifted its head, scenting something new on the air.

That Friday evening when they returned to The Wolf Den, Landon managed, for the most part, to continue to conceal his uneasy feelings. Joy wanted to be there and he wanted Joy to have what she wanted.

Harlon's truck was parked some distance from the house, near a gate that led into the woods. As patrons arrived, they lined the long driveway with their urban vehicles and made their way towards the gate. Despite it being the end of May, there were people wearing scarves and puffy vests and designer toques and fitted gloves. Well prepared, their attire was saying, for an evening in the country.

Harlon had a table set up with a cardboard box for the waivers (which said, in essence, that the signatories were willing witnesses and held Harlon Glen, owner and operator, in no way responsible for any distress they might incur), a cashbox for the fifty-dollar charge, a few rows of plastic cups, and a half-dozen bottles of whisky. Harlon took the money and the waivers. Bill, whom Joy and Landon both recognized as the man from The Heather, stood beside Harlon and poured the complimentary drinks.

Joy went and stood in line while Landon remained by the fire. He watched her. Strangers milled about and sipped their whisky and chatted. There was a nervous energy about them all that Landon noticed. It was an energy that did not help settle him. He wondered if anyone could tell. Joy returned with two cups and handed one to Landon, which he took.

"That man from the restaurant is here," she said. "Bill."

"I saw."

"He's a friend of Harlon's."

"—."

"He seemed—nicer than before."

"—."

Joy touched Landon's arm and looked at him. He felt her eyes making their assessment.

"Here's to us," she said and tapped her plastic cup to his.

He looked at her and tried to smile. They both drank and she rested her head against his chest.

At some distance, standing behind the table, Harlon watched them. He thought Landon looked distracted. He thought Joy looked content. He was thinking this when he realized that Joy was staring at him. He feigned purpose by picking up the stack of waivers and tapping them on the table. When he looked her way again she smiled and waggled the pinky finger of the hand holding her cup. She still had her head on Landon's chest. Landon's eyes were pointed at the woods. Harlon smiled in return and matched Joy's pinky finger wave with a nod and he lifted his cup.

Unknowing, Bill stepped in the way and said something to Harlon. Harlon nodded and climbed into the back of his truck. He stood on the tailgate and held a hand in the air. "Good evening, folks." All eyes turned to him. Even Landon's. "Welcome to Lowbone."

The fire snapped. The air smelled of cedar smoke. The dusklight cast shadows.

"Before we begin, you should know that some of you will have nightmares because of what you see here tonight."

It is not uncommon, Landon, to have nightmares about wolves.

"Some of you may have to hide your eyes or cover your ears."

A few people in the crowd actually covered their eyes and their ears, like they were practising.

It seems to me that you kept returning to the wolves, Landon, as a way of dealing with your nightmares. I think the stillness of the animals must have calmed you.

"Some of you will find you can't look away."

As your doctor I can honestly say that I'm not sure what happened that day you climbed past the barrier in the museum.

"For your own safety, though, don't get too close."

In my estimation you must have had some kind of break. Curling into the mother wolf in the display somehow provided the comfort you were seeking.

"You know, each of us has a wolf somewhere deep within."

Or it might have been an unconscious means of defence. Sometimes getting really close to that which we fear helps mitigate the fear itself and reestablishes a kind of control.

"And a hunger, like an ache."

Harlon's eyes landed on Joy.

Sometimes it isn't distance at all that provides control. Sometimes it's a closeness.

Harlon raised his cup to the crowd and the crowd raised their cups to him.

Everyone drank.

"Welcome to The Wolf Den."

As if on cue, the pack that had for the last fifteen minutes been creeping towards the gate from deep within the woods—

their hunger heightened by the sound of the clucking chickens in the cage and the bantering sounds of the gatherers they'd come to associate with the potentiality of food—set their heads back and howled at the coming night.

At the sudden shrill sound of the six wolves crying out, some within the crowd felt their hearts beat harder. Some covered their mouths. Some covered their eyes and ears as Harlon had predicted. Many jumped back and laughed at themselves nervously. Others, Joy among them, widened their eyes and stepped closer to the fence. Landon remained by the fire, detached now from Joy who seemed pulled by the raw energy of the wolves.

Bill joined Harlon in the back of the truck and they unlatched the cage. Both men reached in and hauled out two live chickens each, holding them in the air for the crowd to see. Then they threw them over the gate. They repeated this ritual three more times.

The chickens batted their wings with everything they had. They hopped around in disarray as the wolves—lips curled, salivating, teeth gnashing—crept closer and closer and closer before falling mercilessly upon them. Within a minute the only sounds beyond the gate were low lupine growls and the sucking and ripping of flesh and the crunching of bone.

When the show was mostly over, the crowd parted. Many formed a line for another shot. Bill climbed down from the truck to pour the drinks and Harlon walked around shaking hands like a politician.

"To the wolves and the whisky," one of the guests shouted. He held the glass high above his head and when he determined enough people were watching him he threw the shot down his throat and slammed the cup on the table like he was a real old-fashioned cowboy: full of grit, the country coursing through his veins.

Everyone was talking about the wolves—how unforgettable they were, how beautiful, how vicious, how unlike anything they had ever seen—and the night had already become a story. Partners posed for pictures to mark the occasion. One woman in a red toque and scarf leaned against a fencepost and held her mittened hands beside her smiling face. A wolf was in the background. In the picture you could see the silhouette of the wolf's head in profile, its one eye. The animal looked like it was staring at the woman. The photo would spin through social media and become the shot of the night.

Landon shoved his hands deep in his pockets and stood beside Harlon's truck. He heard the collection of city vehicles come to life, one engine after the next, and he watched the sets of headlights, like eyes, turn and drive away. He took a breath and held it. When he exhaled he realized he no longer felt uneasy. The voice had calmed him.

Landon watched Joy approach Bill. She touched his shoulder. Bill turned and folded his thick arms over his barrel chest. He nodded and smiled as Joy talked and laughed. Landon took a hand from his pocket and set it on the cold metal hood of the truck. He drummed his fingers. They made almost no sound.

Harlon appeared and smacked the hood a few inches from Landon's hand. "Just so we're clear. She's not for sale."

Harlon sounded like he was joking but Landon wasn't sure. It was dark now and in the dark it was always more difficult to discern not only the message in someone's words but the message in his eyes, particularly a stranger's.

Landon stepped away from the truck and Harlon climbed in and started it. Bill noticed and seemed to relay a pleasant goodbye to Joy. He gathered the whisky bottles and the cups into a box, threw the folding table into the back of the truck, and climbed into the passenger seat. Harlon dropped the truck into gear and drove away. Joy walked up to Landon and slipped her arms around him. She pressed her body against his and set her head again on his chest. He felt the words as she spoke them.

"I love it here," she said. "I don't ever want to leave."

THAT SUMMER IN LOWBONE

—◆◆◆—

The afternoon of the summer solstice Joy walked into town to buy a tin bucket she could fill with ice and chill a bottle of wine in as she lay in the hammock under the tree with a book. Inside the Lowbone Feed & Supply store she found exactly the bucket she had in mind. She also found a pair of rubber boots she had not had in mind and purchased those, too. The boots were bright yellow with black toes and black heels and a big daisy stamped on the side of each. She stood the boots upside down in the bucket, thanked the clerk, and left the store, the bell dinging behind her.

Joy had been walking into town often lately. She liked the smell of the cut hay and the vista of quiet work in the fields. The vehicles that passed her were trucks, mostly, and the drivers always had their windows down, forearms resting on the open frame, one hand on the wheel. They lifted the hand of the resting forearm, these strangers, as they passed her, without taking their eyes from the road. She always raised a hand in return and held it in the air, briefly, after they'd gone.

Usually, Joy's destination was the bookstore. She loved being there. She loved the feeling of the place. She was fond of the paper bags the books came in: TTP stamped on one side, an outline of Dove, the cat, on the other. She really liked talking with Rose. Rose always had something interesting to say. She always had books to recommend. She also knew when to say nothing. *There are things you should know*, Rose had said, but then did not say what those things were. One thing Joy knew too well was that sometimes it didn't take much to ruin the good feelings she had, and as much as she wanted to hear what the things were that Rose thought she and Landon should know, she wanted equally to protect the good feelings that were growing for her here in Lowbone.

After purchasing the tin bucket and the boots she walked into the bookstore like it was her home. The copper bell rang above her. Rose appeared through the beaded curtain in the back, wiping her hands with a tea towel. She smiled when she saw Joy.

Joy smiled in return. She set the bucket and the boots down. She ran a finger along the spines of a row of books as she tilted her head and read the titles.

"So. What are you looking for today?"

"Something with hope, I think. Maybe a little love."

"Neither comes without its difficulties."

Joy turned to Rose. "I would expect no less."

Rose went to a shelf and stood before it, one hand on her hip, the fingers of the other to her lips. She pulled two volumes from the shelf and returned to her station. She stood the books on the counter so Joy could see the covers: *Dance of the Happy Shades* and *No Longer Two People*.

Hugging herself, Joy stepped to the counter and took the two books from Rose. She flipped through the first, then set it down on the counter and flipped through the next.

"That one speaks of the winter that always comes."

Joy looked at Rose like she had just thought of something. Rose waited.

"I hadn't really thought about what winter would be like out here."

"It gets even quieter. Darker, too. The kind of quiet and the kind of dark you cannot imagine until you have lived it."

Dove, the cat, soft-stepped through the curtain in the back, padded toward them, and brushed against Joy's shins on his way toward the windowsill where he slept all afternoon, occasionally raising his head to glimpse someone walking quietly by on the street.

Joy paid for the books and Rose handed her the paper bag that held them.

"We will see you again," Rose said.

"Yes."

"Enjoy the books."

"I will. I look forward to the winter. And the dark."

◆

When Joy left the store she let her mind go to the painting of the wolf she'd been working on that morning and the walk home went by in an instant.

She started up the driveway and waved at Landon who was bent over a worktable he had set up outside the barn. He didn't notice her at first, focused as he was on his work. When she got closer she waved again and this time he saw her. Setting his drawknife on the table, he pocketed his hands and walked towards her.

As the distance between them disappeared Joy held up the paper bag and the tin bucket like she'd won the lottery. She shrugged and laughed which made Landon smile. He took her face in his hands and when he kissed her she let her arms hang heavy at her sides, the paper bag in one hand, the bucket in the other.

"More books," he said.

"More books. And an ice bucket. And boots to work in the garden."

Landon raised his brow. "The garden."

"It can't be that hard."

"Like painting."

She wrinkled her nose. He grinned.

Behind him the barn door was closed. Joy gestured towards it.

"So. Are you making progress on whatever secret thing you've been working on in there and won't show me?"

"I am." He glanced over his shoulder. "And how about you?" He folded his arms. "When do I get to see what you've been up to in that studio of yours?"

Joy stepped past him, grinning. "Who says you get to?"

Landon watched her go. He watched her all the way up the driveway to the house. She did not look over her shoulder once as she went. Only when she had gone up the porch steps and through the door and inside the house, where he could no longer see her, did he move to the table, pick up the drawknife, and return to his work.

◆

On her way through the kitchen Joy slipped a bottle of wine from the rack Landon had made and went to her studio and closed the door. She placed her two new books on the middle shelf of the bookcase. The canoe Landon had carved sat on the top shelf. All of the books she'd purchased since moving to Lowbone were spread out on the shelves, mixed with the ones she had brought with her. Some leaned against one another. Like tired friends, she thought. Like drunk friends. Others lay on their backs in uneven stacks. Like they were sleeping. Like they had given in. She knew the disorder would bother Landon and she pictured him fussing to fix it.

Setting the boots on the windowsill, toe-to-toe so she could see the daisies on the sides, she gazed through the window at the garden. She could name all the flowers and knew the symbolism that attended each, though she had never in her life planted a seed. She uncorked the bottle of wine and drank straight from the mouth. Hugging herself, she assessed the tin bucket she had placed on a small table as though it were a canvas. She tipped the bottle to her mouth again and some of the wine spilled down her chin. She laughed and wiped her face and dried her wine-wet hand on the front of her jeans. She set the bottle down on the windowsill by the boots and went to the door, grabbing the paint-stained apron from the hook. She dropped the apron over her head and tied it around her waist. She flicked through the brushes in the jar that sat on a small table, selected a few, then squeezed some paint onto a palette. Four colours would do it: black to thinly outline the petals, yellow for the petals themselves, white for the pistil, green for the stem and a single leaf. She painted a big daisy on the side of the tin bucket to match the ones on her rubber boots. When she was finished, she spun the bucket around and bit the wooden handle of the brush. She set the brush down and picked up the one dipped in black. On the empty side of the bucket she outlined a big black heart with an arrow piercing it. In the middle of the heart she wrote JK + LW. Assessing her work, she smiled to herself and bit her bottom lip. Then she took off and hung her apron on the hook by the door, rinsed the brushes in a glass of water, and set the brushes up to dry. She took the bottle of wine from the windowsill and *Dance of the Happy Shades* from her shelf and spent the next three hours in the hammock under the tree. She fell asleep. When the late evening breeze woke her the sun was going down. The colour of the sky was burnt orange. She would remember the colour and try to paint that sky. She sat up in the hammock and saw Landon making his way from the barn.

How many perfect days like this one, she thought, could there possibly be?

Sometimes Joy thought about Harlon. Sometimes she dreamt about him. Sometimes she found herself sketching him. Sometimes she found herself wondering what it would be like to dance with him in the dusklight on his porch under the spectre of the coming moon. The press of his body against hers. The press of a whisky kiss. Falling together to the sun-dried sheets of his no-longer-lonely bed.

Sometimes she stopped herself from thinking about Harlon.

Sometimes she did not.

One morning, near the end of June, Joy watched Landon through
her studio window. She was painting. He kept coming into view.
He'd taken a break from whatever secret thing he was working on
in the barn. He was collecting and piling twigs, raking, splitting
wood, turning the earth in the gardens around the flowers he
had planted that spring. She watched him and realized if she
squinted a little and let her focus go he could have been any man.

Joy took up her sketch pad. Standing in front of the window
she drew a series of images. *Man With Rake. Man With Axe. Man
With Spade.* A week later she would use the sketches to paint a
suite of canvases called *Man At Work.* It would be impossible to
tell who the man was in the paintings. Whether she was thinking
about Harlon or Landon or neither or both while she painted
the men she painted didn't matter. Thinking about someone, she
told herself, didn't actually mean anything. Who you imagine
changes nothing. It's who you live with, who you love, who you
touch, who you kiss, who you fall asleep with, who you wake
with in the morning, who you know is there, always, if not in
view then in the periphery, even when it feels like you're alone.
Who is there is what matters. What you imagine isn't even real.

That she sometimes thought about Harlon did not mean she did
not think about Landon. She thought about him all the time. She
thought about him when he sat across from her at the kitchen
table in the morning and he sometimes set the handle of his cup
close to hers. She thought about him in the afternoons in the
hammock when she read. The characters who reminded her of
him. She thought about him when she watched him through her
studio window. When she flipped through the records on the

shelves in the kitchen. As she fell asleep beside him, the backs of her fingers splayed against his ribs. When she woke, aching for him to be inside her. When they lay together, lazy in half-sleep, after.

No, she corrected herself. Thinking about someone does mean something. It has to.

—◆—

Just after one o'clock in the afternoon one day early in July, Landon knocked at her studio door. The knocking was loud and quick and it startled her. When she opened the door she thought Landon looked lost standing there, one hand clutching the back of his neck.

Was she busy, he asked. He knew she was painting, of course, but if she had a few minutes, there was something he'd been meaning to tell her. There was something he thought was probably important. On this particular day at this particular hour he could not seem to get this probably important thing he'd been meaning to tell her out of his head.

"If you've got a moment," he said. "There's something I need to tell you."

Joy, in her journal

How hard it is to really know someone. How much we keep tucked away in the dark corners of our heads. I wish he'd tell me more. I wish he'd tell me everything.

What a terrible thing to have lived through. What a terrible thing to have to remember. How he behaves sometimes makes more sense now. The way he seems to worry at times for no reason at all. The way he can become lost in the middle of a conversation, gone and then back again. The way he stands there sometimes, saying nothing. The way he stares off. The way he stares at me sometimes. The way he talks to himself. He doesn't think I notice but I do. The way he works and works and works, like he's trying to push the day behind him. His attention to detail. His gentleness. The way he loves. How not quite normal he is. How wonderful.

Landon, not quite to himself

So. I told her.

What did she say?

Nothing. She sat there, eyes on me the whole time as I paced back and forth, telling her the story, and she listened. When I stopped talking she looked at me like I was some broken thing she'd let fall from her hands. Then she stood and wrapped her arms around me like she'd just rescued me from freezing water. She held me and said nothing.

What did you do?

I told her I didn't want to get married.

What did she say?

She said she didn't want to get married either.

Same page then.

I told her I did want to do something, though. To mark what we were.

And?

She liked the idea. She liked the word.

The word.

Mark. She said it was fitting.

Like an impression.

Yes. That's it exactly. That's what we're making. An impression.

This is the story Landon told Joy as she sat at the table and
he paced the kitchen floor. Aside from to the man who wore
sweaters, he had never in his life said so much at one time to one
person.

—

I've always been sort of a loner. As long as I can remember.
I've always preferred my own company. My parents worried
about me. They put me in things like Cubs and soccer and I
went along with it. I earned badges. I went on camping trips. I
learned the team cheer and sang along. I gathered in huddles.
Occasionally I scored a goal. I went to season-end parties. But
I always felt something close to relief when I got home and
could just spend time alone in my room, building things and
listening to records.

I did well enough in school and when the time came
my parents wanted me to go away to university. They thought
it would be good for me to leave the nest. I owed it to myself,
they said. I needed to go off on my own and meet people and
experience life and discover who I was.

I didn't want to disappoint them, so I applied. Like most,
I had no idea what I wanted to study or why. On my parents'
advice, I accepted the offer from the school farthest away. It
seemed, they said, like a place suited to me, whatever that meant.
When the time came we drove the four hours without saying
much. Standing outside the residence, suitcase and record player
and a single crate of albums at my feet, we hugged goodbye and
cried a little, like everyone else, and then they told me to go, have
fun, work hard, call if I needed anything.

I spent all of my spare time in the library or my room,
studying or listening to music. I went to class. I took notes. I
wrote the papers. I did well enough.

The only other place where I spent a lot of time was
the museum of natural history. I liked it there. It was quiet.
Everything was still. There was one exhibit—I can't say why—
that I felt really connected to. I felt so connected I went back

every day for ten days in a row. I just stood in front of the exhibit and stared. It was a scene from the wild. A family of wolves. The mother was huddling the pups. The father was in a defensive stance, front forelegs tight to the ground, lips snarling, teeth exposed, eyes gleaming. There was a deer lying behind him, bleeding. The eyes were still open. It was clear the wolves meant to eat the deer. Standing erect in front of the father wolf was a bear. Menacing, growling, front paws raised.

On the tenth day something happened. There was—an incident. That's what the psychologist called it. An incident. Someone from the university phoned my parents. They came to get me. We drove home in the middle of the night. A month or so went by. I told my parents I was fine. But parents know. They know even when kids don't. They asked me if I would go see someone. I said I would. They were worried. I didn't want them to worry. They booked an appointment with someone they knew. I went along. I thought maybe it would help.

It was a beautiful day. My parents seemed happy. They really believed everything was going to be okay. My mom asked if I wanted to sit in the front. I told her no. I knew she liked to be in charge of the radio. Looking up at me, she touched my face and smiled. I think I smiled back. I hope I did. I can still smell the hand cream she always used. Lavender. We climbed into the car and drove away.

Somewhere along the way it happened. The accident. I can't believe that's the word we use. Accident. Anyway, I remember the sun hitting the chrome fender of the car ahead of us. I remember squinting. I remember the oncoming van veering. The suddenness of the impact. I remember the feeling of being thrown forward while the seatbelt held me like it meant never to let me go. I remember not being able to breathe. I remember the green digits of the dashboard clock somehow suddenly inches from my face and blinking. 1:07. 1:07. 1:07.

Everything happened so fast. So slow.

When I got my breath back I tried to move but couldn't. The seatbelt had me locked and the back of the driver's seat pressed against my legs. I could see the back of Mom's head. She wasn't moving. Neither was Dad. I tried to speak but the words would not come.

So I listened.

"Run On For a Long Time" was playing on the radio.

All I could hear was the music and my parents breathing.

Then, only the music.

I remember the sudden sun in my eyes and the rush of cold air on my face. It didn't take the firefighters long to tear a hole in the roof of the car. I remember not wanting to leave. I remember squeezing my eyes shut like I could undo it all if only I thought hard enough. I remember the scented pinecone Mom had made and hung from the rearview mirror somehow being in my lap. I remember closing my hand around it. I remember the feeling of being pulled through the hole in the roof knowing that I would never be in that place, or any other place, with those two people again.

ASSURANCES

❖❖❖

Three days later.

As the sun began its descent below the cedar woods and the loons made their evening calls on the river, Landon brought his mother's record player out to the porch and lowered the arm. The needle made a scratching sound and the song began. Joy followed, barefooted on the porch, with a bottle of Valpolicella and two glasses dangling between her fingers by the stems. She had painted her toes and fingernails an earthy green and wore a long spaghetti-strap sundress of the same colour. She had pinned a daisy to the thin braid in her sun-lightened copper hair. Landon wore jeans and a loose-fitting white linen shirt. His brown leather boots were scuffed but scrubbed clean. Joy uncorked the bottle and poured. They clinked glasses and drank. They faced each other and smiled and their smiles fell to laughter. They quietened and took each other's hands. They stood there and listened to the music. The piano softly wept and the trumpet sighed as the troubadour sang about the swallows in the steeple and his own hollow dreams.

"Joy. It is my assurance to discover with you, and fix in place as we do, the components of a life we come to live, separately and together, and in that way what we come to build will be solid and strong and sure."

He slipped the plain wooden ring he had made for her onto the pinky finger of her right hand. Joy looked at the ring. She turned it with her thumb.

"Landon. It is my assurance to discover with you the painting of our life. On whatever wall the painting eventually hangs I hope we can stand back and look at it together."

Joy went on her toes and fixed a daisy in Landon's hair. She fell back on her heels and assessed her work. The flower fell out of Landon's hair but he caught it in his hands. He tucked the daisy behind his ear and Joy went on her toes again to kiss him. Darkness descended around them and the sound of the piano and the trumpet faded and the last words of the song fell with the sun, sad-sounding and strained and beautiful.

FINISHED, COMPLETE

—◆◆◆—

Two days later Landon stood in the barn, arms folded, and looked at what he had built. It had taken him the better part of a month, ten hours a day. He stepped outside the barn and shielded his eyes against the brightness, the sun at its apex in a pristinely blue July sky. He breathed the warm summer air in and held it, exhaled, and walked up to the house, kicking the odd stone as he went, hands pocketed like a drifter.

Inside her studio Joy heard the screen door snap shut. She set her brush down, hung her apron on the hook by the door, and assessed her own work. A dozen canvases stood around the room, some leaning against the walls, some on easels Landon had made. She had been working steadily since the beginning of May. She touched her lips with a single finger. What she had accomplished seemed complete. *Complete* was the word. *Complete* was different from *finished*.

She spoke to the quiet room, a familiar restlessness slipping in around her. "So. What now, Joy? What now?"

She turned the wooden ring on her finger. Her eyes landed on the painting of the wolf. She thought of Harlon. She was thinking about Harlon a lot.

It was happening again. She was defenceless against it.

Why did there always have to be something else? Why couldn't she just be happy? What was she looking for? What, in the end, would be the thing to make her stay?

◆

When Joy came into the kitchen, Landon was busy at the counter, making lunch: thickly sliced bread slathered with salted butter, cubes of old cheddar, dark coffee. Joy scanned the albums on the shelves Landon had made. She settled on *Sweet Forgiveness* and set it to play. She closed her eyes, nodded to the beat, and began to turn—arms spread, head down—around the kitchen floor. An easy free verse shamble around the room.

Near the end of the opening song, "About To Make Me Leave Home," Landon took the two plates he'd readied to the table. Joy spun her way to the counter, poured two cups of the dark coffee, and danced her way to the table without spilling a drop.

They ate without a word, as they often did, and listened to the soundtrack of this particular midday: "Runaway," then "Two Lives," and then the next song and then the next. At the end of the title track, Landon went to the record player and turned the volume down. He leaned against the wall there, folded his arms, and crossed his ankles.

"I have some news."

Joy took a mouthful of coffee and held it before she swallowed. "You're through working on whatever secret thing you've been working on out there in the barn."

"How did you know that?"

She told him she was standing at her open window, staring out.

Landon furrowed his brow. He wondered for a moment whether Joy could actually see him from the window in her studio.

She said she could hear the wind blow, touching the restless day.

Landon clued in. Her words were the lyrics of the song he had turned down, "My Opening Farewell."

"Clever. As always." He pushed himself from the wall and dropped his hands in his pockets. "And how about you. Are you finished?"

"*Finished* is not the word, Landon." She pretended to catch something in the air. She shook the fist that held the invisible thing she had pretended to catch and blew on it. Then she opened the fist one finger at a time and pretended to watch a butterfly flutter away. "But with a bit of magic I do think some of my paintings—maybe all of them—are complete."

"—."

"You're wondering. What the difference is."

"—."

She took him by the wrist and walked him to her studio, his arm like a tether to his body.

"*Complete* refers to the idea of something being full or rounded out," she said. "Like filling a bucket."

Landon thought of the stone well and the wooden bucket that went with it.

Joy thought of the tin bucket she'd painted a daisy on.

"Or," she said, "in my case, a canvas."

She reached out for the antique lever-handle Landon had installed on her studio door and pressed down on the arm.

"*Finished*," she said, turning to look at him, "refers, rather bleakly, to the end of something. Like a song." She pushed open the door and Landon's eyes went straight to the middle of the room where the painting of the wolf stood, its leery-eyed face taking up the whole canvas. "Or a day," she said, "Or a life. Or a love."

—◆—

Landon entered the studio and stood in front of the painting. Joy waited. Landon did not say anything. She wondered if it was possible that he didn't like what he saw. Had she really spent all these mornings, all these hours, all these days in here, and this—this is all she had done?

She stepped between him and the painting and reached up and took his face in her hands.

"Tell me. Tell me what you think."

He took her wrists and gently pulled her hands away. He breathed deeply in and held it. She watched him. Eventually he exhaled like it was the end of all things and looked past her into the eyes of the wolf.

"Tell me," she said, falling back on her heels, nearly giving in.

He stared at the painting. "It looks so. Real."

—◆—

Joy hugged herself with both arms and watched Landon walk around the room. He squatted in front of the pieces leaning against the walls and set his face so close to them he could smell the paint. He poked one canvas like he might actually be able to dip his finger in the river water she had painted, like he might actually be able to feel the silky wetness of the lily pads. He ran his fingertips lightly over another painting, thinking the dusklighted wood of the barn in the picture might feel like the dusklighted wood of the barn he worked in. He noted the zoomed-in portrait of the copper bell from above the bookstore door. She had somehow made the verdigris look powdered and layered on the bell's surface. He touched it with his middle finger and then felt the middle finger with his thumb.

"They're all from here. Our house. The woods. The river. The town. As the sun is setting or coming up or gone completely. And this one," he said, looking again at the wolf.

Joy touched her lips. "I know."

They looked at the wolf for a while and then Landon indicated three canvases by the window. The suite Joy called *Man At Work*. "Are these meant to be me?"

"They're you. They're also not you."

She moved to a table where she kept a jar of brushes.

He watched her.

She ran her palm across the collection of bristles. She plucked a brush from the jar and waved it in front of him like a wand. She touched his forehead with it, his nose, his chin. She touched the handle-end of the brush in the hollow at the base of his throat and drew a slow but heavy line down his chest to his abdomen and tapped the top of his belt buckle three times before slipping the length of the brush behind the buckle and pulling her body into his.

"I'm happy you like my paintings."

"I'm happy you're happy."

She touched his face. He looked at her. He could not tell what she was thinking.

"Happy is a good thing to be."

---◆---

Joy slipped into her jeans and her shirt in a single breath.

Landon remained on the floor. He opened his eyes and there she was: one hand on her hip, the other holding a paintbrush like a cigarette. She blew pretend smoke to the ceiling and stepped over him. He stood and fumbled a bit with his clothes.

Dressed, he patted his back pockets like he was missing something and looked around like a lost man.

"This way," Joy said, standing in the doorway, grinning, holding out a hand for him to take.

He went to her. He took the hand. She shut off the light and hooked a finger over the lever handle. The door clicked closed behind them as they went.

---◆---

Inside the barn, Joy ran a finger along the gunwale of the cedar strip canoe. She stepped the length of the boat from stern to bow, tracing her pinky finger along the wood, eyes trained on all the detail.

"I thought with the river and all."

Joy took three slow steps towards Landon, slipped her arms around his waist, and set her face against his chest. He held her softly and kissed the top of her head. Her hair, like always, smelled like wool.

A barn swallow batted its wings above them, desperate, it seemed, to find its way out.

"I love it," Joy murmured, and Landon thought she might be crying.

WHAT NOW

—◆◆◆—

July went by in a blink. Joy painted the mornings away. She thought about Harlon. She thought about Landon. She ate bread and cheese and drank coffee and wine. She lounged in the hammock and fell asleep there, dreaming herself into the novels she read. She walked into town and talked with Rose. She bought more books and collected the paper bags they came in. She bought a floppy straw hat with a wide brim like a wave. On her return from town she quoted lines from her favourite novels out loud: to herself, to the trees, to the animals within the woods. She felt, she had to admit, like she was on her way home. She felt, she had to admit, like she was lost and did not know which way to go.

—◆—

Joy took the yellow rubber boots from the windowsill in her studio one morning and pulled them on. She sat on the sill and assessed the boots on her feet. With a fingertip she traced the daisy on the side of each boot. Then she stood and went outside, filled a watering can from the hose, and stepped along the edge of the flower garden. Fat drops fell softly from the watering can's wide metal spout, wetting the petals and the leaves and the stems and the garden's dark tilled earth. Joy named the flowers as the water drops hit them, as if she were some kind of flower god pronouncing them into existence.

—◆—

Late in the afternoon one day near the end of July, Joy walked the trail through the cedar woods and emerged to find the canoe Landon had made leaning against a stand by the river. Landon had portaged the boat through the trail and said it would be waiting for her when she felt like she wanted to give it a try. Joy touched the hull and held her palm there. It felt cool and smooth and real. She lowered the boat to the ground and pulled the bow into the water. Stepped from the dock into the boat and sat. Took up the paddle Landon had carved her and reached the blade of the paddle beyond a lily pad she did not want to disturb and pulled. Reached and pulled. For the first time in her life she was in a canoe, paddling, alive with the feel of it, communing with the croaking frogs, the flitting insects, the water birds, the fish whose dark silhouettes she sometimes saw in her periphery, like ghosts in the green water, there and then gone in a flash. She breathed in the still summer air and the clean, rich, warm water smells. She watched a great blue heron lift from its secret perch amidst the tall grasses, silent and unreal-seeming. "Hello, little dragon," she said, paddling down the river like a dream she thought might go on forever.

Sometime later, on her return, the air had become cooler and the sun was low in the sky. Shadows fell all around and she raised a hand to who she thought must be Landon standing on their dock in the distance, silhouetted in the falling dark, hands pocketed, still. Not wanting to break the serenity, she did not call out. She continued to reach and pull the blade of the paddle through the water, steering the bow into shore. When she pulled the boat into the dock, Landon was gone, and she wondered if he had been there at all.

Joy climbed out of the boat and hauled it by the bow up the bank and onto the grassy shore. With a heave and a little struggle she stood the boat against its stand. She shivered as a breeze lifted and swirled about her, cooler than it should have been for an evening in late July. In the distance a wolf howled, which was not uncommon, but the suddenness and the sharpness of the call and the feeling of it made her gasp and turn her head. She took in the sight of the river once more before leaving and in the growing dark she thought it looked like something from a myth. She thought of a title: *Styx at Dusk.*

Joy, in her journal

The last page. Volume One, a recap.

The man who a paternity test would say was my father was gone from my life before I was born, lost forever in the shadows of his leaving. The woman who was more like an estranged sister than a mother was mostly absent too. Growing up I spent a lot of time alone. By the time I turned ten I fended mostly for myself. It wasn't uncommon that I woke to an empty house or came home to an empty house. I'm not complaining. I really didn't mind it. When I think about it, I don't think I would have wanted it any other way. I came to love the independence. When I turned eighteen mommy-dearest hugged me like I was someone she met for coffee once a month and bid me adieu. She was finally off to see the world, she said, on her own. I decided then that leaving must be in the family genes, and so when she set off to see the world I decided to venture off myself. I haven't stopped since. As clear as it is that I'm not the settling-down type, it is clear that Landon is. It's not hard to see that. I don't want to hurt him. I really don't. But I've been thinking a lot about Harlon. I wonder if he's been thinking about me.

—

Sometimes, when I dream, what I dream becomes real. I dreamed of Victoria before I met her. I saw the kanji tattoo behind her ear. I couldn't see her face but I heard her voice in the dream. I heard her whisper that the tattoo meant love. I saw the tortoise shell ring I bought her in the market the

day we met. I saw her in the bed the morning
after the night I was gone, waking alone to the
note I left on the pillow. I dreamed of Sophie's and
Michel's little girl, Rebecca, before I met either of
them. I saw her in a daisy dress, spinning a hula-
hoop on her hips. I dreamed of Silke's scarf and
the bars in Berlin. I dreamed of Sly. I dreamed
of the empty room he was squatting in and
took me to. I dreamed of the jacaranda trees in
Johannesburg. And I always dreamed of leaving
before I actually did. I foresaw the note I wrote
every time: I tried. I'm sorry. I love you. Goodbye.

—

I want to be clear: I'm not bored out here in
the country. I thought I might be. I thought being
bored might be the thing to ruin it. I thought
being bored might be the thing to make me leave.
But how could I be bored with all those canvases
to paint, all those flowers to tend to, all those
records to play, all that wine to drink, all those
novels to read. How could I be bored with my
very own River Styx to paddle and a ghost to call
my own.

The first time I saw the ghost I thought the
ghost was Landon. I thought maybe my mind was
playing tricks on me. And maybe it was. Maybe it
is. But I've seen him a few times now, my ghost.
When the light goes low and I'm paddling back
into shore. He's there and then he's not. Gone
like a whisper. Like something plucked from
Walpole or Shelley. A story wherein the spirit of
a long-dead woodsman appears every night by
the water where he was last seen, resting a long-

handled axe on his shoulder. A hard-working
young carpenter and his free-spirited young wife
purchase the woodsman's long-abandoned home.
In the evening the young wife paddles the river.
The ghost of the woodsman appears and at first
the young wife is not sure, but she's curious so she
returns every evening and one night there's no
mistaking it. The ghost is a ghost and it silently
instructs her. She undresses, takes the anchor
from the boat rubbing against the dock in the
water, and ties the anchor to her ankle. The ghost
hovers above the river, beckoning her. She picks
up the anchor and as she drops it off the end of
the dock she steps with it, her body gone in a
blurp. In the morning the young carpenter wakes
with a start and all he finds of his young wife is
a note: I tried. I'm sorry. I love you. Goodbye.
When he comes barrelling through the woods he
halts at the sight of what awaits him on the dock:
her dress neatly folded, her sandals, her hat, her
ring, and, inexplicably, an old long-handled axe.

How haunting. How delightful.

I wonder what Harlon would think. There's
something of a ghost in the howl of a wolf.

—

I had a dream last night that I found an old
wooden box on a shelf in the corner of the
basement of this old house with a leather journal
inside it. As I opened the journal I woke, a shiver
running through me.

—

When I finish this page I will close this
journal (maybe forever) and paint all morning in
a studio Landon built me in a house we bought
together in the country. Where the only people
I see are a bookseller named Rose, a waitress
named Esther, on occasion a man named
Bill, Harlon in my dreams, and Landon in the
everyday waking of my life.

I can't help but wonder if this might be it. I
can't help but wonder what else there might be.

A PHONE CALL & A STORY

—◆◆◆—

August 1st.

Joy looked for Landon but could not find him, which was strange. There were only so many places he could be.

She checked the basement. The stairs creaked beneath her. At the bottom of the stairs she flicked the switch a few times. No lights came on. Landon said he was going to replace the bulbs but obviously had not. The concrete floor was cold and the low joist-exposed ceiling was heavy with cobwebs. The basement, smaller than her studio, smelled of oil and metal and dust and rags. It was dark. A sliver of light slipped in through the one small window. She walked to the far corner and there, like it was waiting for her, was the box she had seen in her dream. There was a latch on the box with a small key-lock. Joy pinched the lock and tugged on it. The lock itself wasn't that big. She found an old heavy wrench. She lifted the wrench a few inches above the lock and struck it. She tried again. On the third blow the lock released. She set the wrench down, flipped the latch, and lifted the lid.

She slid both hands under the journal and lifted it out like it might come apart in her hands. Two old chairs were stacked under the small window. She worked one of the chairs free and sat on it. Unwrapped the journal's leather strap, carefully, as if it were a bandage. Flipped through the mostly blank pages. On the first page there was an inscription:

To Molly,

upon the occasion of our still being here

With much love, yours in perpetuity,

Robert

On the next page, halfway down, was what looked like the beginning of a story, the writing of which was markedly different from the inscription's. There was a title centred a few lines above the first indented sentence. Joy decided the story, if that's what it was, must have been written by the woman named Molly. She wondered what had happened to her. How she up and disappeared, as Marty had said. Whatever had happened, this journal had been kept in this old wooden box on purpose. Like a marker of some kind. A testament. A warning.

Whatever it meant, Joy wanted to know.

She opened the journal and started to read.

Nightsounds

The phone rings and it wakes me.

I'm asleep and then I'm not.

It's the middle of the night in the dead of winter and I'm alone in this old house in the country in the dark.

Unless he's come back.

It didn't used to be like this. For years, everything was fine. We were happy. Or so I thought. He worked too much, but that was the life he inherited. It's the life I signed up for. I knew that. I used to kid him. You'll dig an early grave for yourself working that hard. Ah, Molly, he'd say. No grave is early. It's only ever on time. He smiled when he said this. I smiled in return. A dark sense of humour we shared.

But then he got quiet. Really quiet. He started working more. So much I barely saw him. And then one day he was gone. I thought something had happened. I called the police to report him missing but they told me not to worry. Husbands did that sometimes. Did what, I asked. Don't worry, they said. He'll be back.

Then he was. And things were fine again. For a while. Fine, if not good. And then, slowly, the pattern started all over. He got quieter and quieter and quieter. He stayed in the barn until all hours. He slept out there some nights. I found him one morning asleep in a stall. I woke him and he looked up at me, eyes all ablaze. He jumped up like he was late for something and without a word he was gone again. Days later, he came home in the middle of the night. He was standing at the foot of the bed. I woke with a start and he looked at me and then he left the room. In the morning he was at the table, drinking coffee, like nothing had happened. I sat with him. He poured me a cup. We looked at each other. He smiled. He told me he loved me. He told me he always would.

He's been gone for a while this time. I've lost count of the days. I don't know if he's coming back. I don't know if I want him to.

The phone rings.

I blink hard. My heart thumps in my chest, in my head, in the pads of my thumbs. I do not move. Not even my toes against the tightly tucked sheets at the end of the bed.

Old houses like this one come alive at night when the world lies still.

The creak of the floors, the wind in the shutters, the drip of old faucets.

The low rumble of the furnace coming on like far away thunder ignited.

The night sounds of winter that find their way in through the cracks and old windows of old houses like this one. The ground, frozen and splitting. Some nocturnal animal, foraging: the teeth crunching old insects from the underside of a fallen tree, nails clawing at the bark, the punky pulp.

There.

The hollow sound of a single breath. Like a sigh.

I was sleeping and now I'm not and I hear someone breathing.

The phone rings again.

My eyes go from the window to the bedroom door. To the handle. It's the only movement I make.

In the dream, before I woke, I was sitting on the ground, legs crossed, watching a wolf gnaw on a bone. I wanted to reach out and take the bone. I wanted to reach out and touch the dark curl of the wolf's lip. I wanted to feel the heat of its breath. When the wolf looked up its eyes were empty but intent, watching me but not. One of my arms was missing, which didn't seem to bother me. My one hand held the shoulder where my other arm should've been. There was no blood. Only a white bone in the black night pinned to the cold ground by the paws of a grey wolf gnawing.

Runh. Runh. Runh.

I realized the bone the wolf was working on was mine, the humerus. Clean and white and perfect. In a thousand years someone in this dreamworld would unearth it and document the length and the girth and calculate the age and speculate about the teeth marks. The bone would tell a story.

Maybe it's a wolf with a bone I hear outside my window right now.

In the dream the gnawing became a warning—Runh. Runh. RUN—which became the sound of the phone ringing.

And then I woke up.

The phone rang and now I am lying here, eyes wide open and straining, waiting for the next ring.

I will it. Which somehow feels like control.

Ring, I whisper. Ring.

And so it comes.

That was the third one.

There will be five before the machine clicks in.

I strain.

The breathing again. Maybe it's the wind. Maybe it's him.

I lie here, clutching the comforter to my chin like a child scared of the monsters in the closet.

Someone is in the house.

I can hear footsteps in the kitchen.

No, it's not footsteps. It's the plastic tassel clicking against the slatted blinds of the window at the end of the hall. I can see it. The tassel. Snapping against the slats.

Click, click. Click.

The phone rings.

My eyes hurt. The alarm clock on my dresser's too far away to read.

The clicking becomes a tapping and the tapping is in the room. A fingernail against the windowpane.

Tap, tap. Tap.

I cannot see the hand it's attached to or the face pressed against the window looking in. It's too dark. The clouds and the snow coming down dull the light of the moon. If the night were clear I could see by the moonlight and then I would know.

I would know no one was there. I would know it wasn't him.

Maybe it's the branch of the tree outside my window, moving in the wind, tapping the window like a fingernail.

Get up. Get up and then you'll know.

The phone rings.

I wait for the machine to click in and when it does I hear a child's voice and because it's so young and so sweet and so light and so airy I cannot tell if it's a boy or a girl:

We are not here right now

We are not home

Please leave a message

After the tone

If you want to talk to us

Say who you are

And oh—no—don't worry

We haven't gone far

I try to hear the voice of who is calling. I try to hear if it's him.

Only breathing. Then a dial tone.

The echo of the child's voice sounds in my head (haven't gone far—gone far—gone far) and I cannot understand why it's a child's voice when I have no children of my own.

If I get out of bed and turn on the light I will see that no one is there. But sometimes people who hear nightsounds when they're all alone in the dark get out of bed and turn on the lights only to discover they are not alone.

There are stories.

There are stories of intruders—of people you know, of people you know very well—slipping in through the bedroom doors, standing at the foot of the bed, still, smirking, lips curled like a wolf's in a dream. A shushing finger to those lips.

There are stories that don't end well.

Shhh. Listen.

What was that?

The front door clicking shut.

Slow footsteps in the hall.

I sit up. I watch the bedroom door. The handle turns.

I am not alone.

The next day the phone rang in the kitchen and Landon answered it.

"Mr. Wood?"

"This is Landon Wood. Who is this?"

"Who is this, he says. With an air of suspicion. A touch of worry maybe. Which is it, Mr. Wood, suspicion or worry? Have you done something wicked? Are you worried that you might?"

Landon furrowed his brow. He was about to hang up when he heard the woman on the other end of the line laughing, not derisively. Her laugh reminded him of Joy's laugh.

"Mr. Wood?"

"Yes."

"You're still there. Excellent. I was only teasing."

"Is there something I can help you with?"

"A man of few words and straight to the point. I respect that. And yes, there is something you can help me with. I am standing in a store called Naturalis where I have just purchased a coat rack you created, and I have to say it is the most exquisite coat rack I have ever seen. It should be the benchmark for all future coat racks."

Landon wasn't sure how a coat rack of all things could provoke such a reaction. He also thought *created* was a strange word to use.

"I'm not sure what to say."

"Thank you would be a start. I essentially called you the paragon of your craft. Believe me, in my line of work that is no small gesture."

"Okay. Thank you."

"You are welcome. Now, back to business, which in my case is art. I own and run a highly successful gallery downtown called *Fuse!*—perhaps you've heard of it."

"I don't know much about art."

"Nonsense. You are an artist yourself."

"That's very kind of you but—"

"Forget politeness, Mr. Wood. Politeness is weakness."

"I don't know if that's true, but I think it's Joy you want to speak with."

"Who is Joy?"

"The woman I live with. She's the artist."

"Is she. Well, we shall see. In the meantime, I need you to create twenty easels in the style of the coat rack I have just purchased. What is the wood, red cedar?"

Landon was impressed. "Yes."

"I need them by the middle of September. That's six weeks from now exactly. I will pick them up myself. I will meet this Joy you speak of and assess her work. You have piqued my interest."

"She'll be excited."

"Or devastated if I crush her dreams. Which is more likely the case."

Landon wasn't sure if this last part was a statement or a question.

"The likelihood of discovering two artists under one roof is slim, Mr. Wood. At best."

"Well. Like I said, she's the artist."

"And like I said, we shall see. Now, where do you live?"

"Lowbone."

"Lowbone. My god, it sounds like something from a Clint Eastwood movie."

"That describes it pretty well."

"I'll be sure to wear a hat and bring a flask."

"—."

"Declan, my driver, will look up this Lowbone of yours and we will see you smack dab in the middle of September. Don't disappoint me, Mr. Wood."

"I'll do my best."

"Yes. You will."

"Goodbye, Mrs.—"

"My name is Cynthia Vale. My friends call me Synth. My enemies call me Sin. Take your pick, but for the love of all things dark and mysterious please do not call me Mrs. I am unmarried and am determined to remain so."

Landon heard *damned determined*.

"Okay. Cynthia. I appreciate the call."

"The appreciation, Mr. Wood, is all mine."

Cynthia Vale pressed the red circle on her cellphone and left the store with a flourish.

Standing in the kitchen, Landon looked at the old-fashioned receiver in his hand and returned it to its cradle.

—◆—

Joy was in her studio rereading Molly's story. She had heard the phone ring. She had heard the sounds of Landon talking. She had heard the sounds of his talking stop. They didn't get many phone calls. When she was finished reading, Joy closed Molly's journal. Holding it to her chest she went to the kitchen.

Landon was leaning against the counter with a coffee, listening to the Johnny Cash song. He hadn't played it in a while. He thought he might cut down a cedar or two and have them milled for the easels Cynthia Vale had commissioned. The phrase *cut down* had made him think of the song, and then he had wanted to hear it. When Joy came into the kitchen he went to the record player and turned it off. They both sat at the table and looked at each other.

Landon told Joy about the phone call. Joy widened her eyes at the mention of Cynthia Vale's name. She knew who she was, of course. Landon told her what Cynthia Vale had said about coming here, to their home. To meet Joy. To see her work.

Joy leaned forward in her chair. "Are you serious?"

"I am. She said she's coming smack dab in the middle of September to pick up the easels she wants me to make and to see your work. Those were her words."

"To see my work."

"That's what she said. Yes."

Joy's shoulders fell.

Landon watched her. She did not blink. She looked lost, and happy being so. A hint of a smile rose at one corner of her mouth.

"Okay," he said. "Your turn."

Her eyes met his. "My turn."

He pointed at the journal in her lap. "You bought a new journal. It looks old."

She looked at the journal and placed a hand on top of it. "It is old. But I didn't buy it. I found it here. In the basement."

Landon thought about the word *basement.*

About what the word *base* meant.

A foundation. To ground. To situate as the centre.

Inferior, ignoble, reprehensible.

"I think what's on these pages," Joy said, tapping the journal, "has something to do with, you know—"

Her voice fell to a whisper.

"—what *happened* here."

Landon sat back in his chair.

She held the journal out to him. "Do you want to read it?"

Landon folded his arms like he was thinking. Like he was cold. He glanced towards the top of the stairs leading to the basement.

"No. I don't think that I do."

Landon, not only to himself

Well. You're quiet today.

I'm thinking.

What about?

I don't know.

You can tell me. You can tell me anything.

I'm thinking that I like it here.

In this room, you mean.

Yes. This room. This house. This town.

It's quiet, isn't it.

It is. I like that Joy is here. I like that you are here.

It's nice to have someone to talk to.

It is. Having someone to talk to is something I have not had in a really long time.

PURPOSEFUL LANGUOR

—◆◆◆—

Early one morning a week or so later, Landon woke in the darkness. He turned his head on the pillow and watched Joy sleep. Her brow knit, her lips pressed together, the corners of her mouth pointed down like little arrows, the blankets clutched tightly in her fists under her chin. He wished he could see what she saw in her dreams. He wanted to know what her mind made of their life when she wasn't in control of the images or the words. What did she see, he wanted to know, in the still, quiet hours of the dark?

—◆—

That evening they sat on the porch and Joy made note of the light in the sky as it went from gold to copper to crimson. They were most of the way through a bottle of Valpolicella, listening to an album called *Whereabouts*. Many of their days culminated this way: a purposeful languor. They sipped and listened to Ron Sexsmith as the dusklight fell around them and a late summer coolness whispered of the season's end.

"Do you ever wonder," she said, "about all of the things we miss and all of the people we never know because at every given moment we are where we are and not someplace else?"

It was the last thing Landon would ever wonder and he wasn't sure how she didn't know that.

"No," he said. "No, I don't."

"Why did you want to leave the city?"

He pictured his parents' house. His father's parents' house. It had been in the family a long time.

"I'd lived with their ghosts long enough."

The word *ghosts* made Joy think of her own ghost on the dock by the river. He was becoming a painting in her mind.

"But why here?"

"I wanted night skies I could see stars in without trying. I wanted space. I wanted country air." He breathed in and held it, stretched out his arms, looked up at the sky. He exhaled. "I wanted quiet."

"It is quiet." Joy sipped her wine. "What Rose said makes sense. I know what she means now."

"—."

"Remember? She said, nothing ever happens in Lowbone, but it always feels like something might. I like that."

Landon set his glass to his lips.

Joy looked out over the porch rail. "If you could do anything, what would it be?"

Landon stared off into the distance. Then he turned to her and quoted the lyrics of the song they were listening to. He told her there was nothing he'd rather do than sit there and talk with her. A beautiful view.

Joy smiled and sipped her wine and looked at him. He never asked her questions like the ones she had just asked him, and she wondered how he could not know how much she wanted him to.

Joy, in Molly's journal

Settled. Like a sunflower hanging its head in the evening, tired from a day of looking up. Like the stillness of a freshly cleaned blanket that has been snapped above a bed like a matador's cape. Like sediment resting in layers at the bottom of a river. Some days I feel like that sunflower. Some days I feel like I'm under that blanket. Some days I feel like I'm at the bottom of that river.

Landon, not only to himself

You look like you want to tell me something.

There's this woman, Cynthia Vale.

Who's that?

She owns an art gallery. In the city.

Okay.

She has me making easels for her.

That sounds good.

It's fine. She's going to look at Joy's art.

That sounds good, too.

It is. It's just. I don't know. She seems different.

As any one person is.

I mean it feels like something is about to happen.

Like what?

Something I can't control.

Deep breaths.

I know, but I don't think that will help this time.

Why?

I can feel it coming.

Feel what coming?

There's no way of knowing for sure. But something. Something is coming.

I don't think you should worry. Try to forget it.

How can I forget something that hasn't happened yet?

—◆—

The last day in August, summer's end, and the sun was beginning its slow slide in a jewel-blue sky. Joy had painted all morning and now she was in the hammock under the tree with her tin bucket half full of ice, a bottle of wine, and a novel about the last woman on earth. Sometime in the late afternoon she fell asleep. The book lay open on her chest like a shield.

She woke at dusk, the umber sun sinking, the moon full, like an eye, above the cedar woods. Landon was standing over her. Joy rubbed her eyes. She held out a hand for Landon to take and he did. An evening breeze blew through the leaves of the tree above her. She smiled.

"They're trying to tell us something," she said. "If you listen hard enough you can hear them, all those tiny creatures we cannot see." She looked at him. "They're everywhere, you know. You only have to listen."

SOMEONE ELSE

✦✦✦

Seeptember 15th, noon.

Joy and Landon had just finished lunch and they were listening to *The Fate of the World Depends on This Kiss*. Rinsing his cup and plate, Landon looked out the kitchen window and in the distance saw a white van turn up the driveway.

"She's here."

Joy brought her dishes to the sink and stood at Landon's shoulder, watching through the window as the van approached the house. "What do you think she's like?"

"I really don't know."

"What did she sound like?"

"Confident. She used words like *shall* and *exquisite*. She said Lowbone sounded like something from a Clint Eastwood movie."

"I'm nervous."

Landon looked at her.

"People think art is so subjective but it's really not. Good is good. No monkey can write a novel and if an elephant paints a picture it might be cute but they don't hang cute in the Louvre."

"Well. I don't know anything about any of that. But I know you can paint."

She placed a hand on his chest. "You're so good. I'm so lucky and you're so good." She took him by the hand and started for the door. "Let's go meet Cynthia Vale."

◆

Cynthia Vale stepped down from the van wearing black ballet flats, a high-waisted white jumpsuit, a black wide-brimmed floppy hat, and a white silk scarf. Her eyes were the kind of blue that looked fake, but no one would ever know because no one would ever ask.

"Isn't this exquisite," she said, indicating the ivory cigarette holder she held between two fingers, stepping toward Landon and Joy like a model on the catwalk. "It was Natalie Wood's, you know. I fell in love with it the moment I saw it. I leapt from my seat at the auction, number card thrust as high as I could reach it. No one bid against me but the minimum was high enough, let me tell you." She winked at Joy. "How could I fall so headlong in love with something like a cigarette holder, you might ask, especially when I don't smoke? Fair question. But I mean, just look at it. You can almost smell the history."

She ran the length of the holder under her nose. She walked a circle around Landon and Joy, taking in the porch and the expanse of the property as she did. "Just think, when I place it in my lips, it's like my lips are touching the lips of Natalie Wood, whose lips touched the lips of James Dean. Could you imagine touching your lips to more beautiful lips than the lips of Natalie Wood or James Dean?"

She paused for a moment and looked at Landon and Joy. "You both have beautiful lips. I bet when you kiss it is something to see."

Joy bit the end of her pinky finger, the one with the wooden ring. She was beaming.

Cynthia Vale examined the cigarette holder in her hand. "There is a kind of mystery here. Like in her death. I can sense it. I can sense many things. I would love my own death to be as mysterious as hers. Wouldn't you? Not that I'd want to drown. There can be nothing elegant about drowning. Unless you can manage it the way Ophelia does, singing all the while, decorated with flowers, succumbing peacefully to muddy death. But who's to know what happened *really*? The singing was probably fabricated. It is, after all, reported by the treasonous Queen. And how can any drowning be peaceful? The only way we come to understand the peace of Ophelia's end is through the paintings. Like Millais's. Paintings give us everything, don't you think? If we're to know the truth of it, poor Ophelia likely flailed." Cynthia Vale looked directly at Joy. "Whatever happens, my dear, I will not flail."

She placed the cigarette holder between her lips and drew on it. There was no smoke because there was no cigarette. She seemed to be finished her speech.

Turning her attention to Landon she reached out and tapped his cheek. "You. You're exactly as I imagined. Tall, handsome, a little rough around the edges. Tell me, did you finish my easels?"

"I did."

"Excellent. Be a dear, will you, and show Declan here where they are."

Declan, the driver, was standing beside the van awaiting instruction. He wore a dark sports jacket and tie. His silver hair was cropped. His shoulders were wide. A driver, thought Landon, and a bodyguard in one. Landon acknowledged him and Declan nodded in turn.

Landon gestured towards the barn. Declan opened the driver's side door and as he climbed into his seat he motioned for Landon to join him, which Landon did.

Cynthia and Joy watched the van go.

"Mr. Wood tells me you paint."

Joy tucked her hair and slipped her hands into her back pockets. "I do."

Cynthia Vale looked at her and made a flourish with the hand holding the cigarette holder. "Show me."

While Landon and Declan went to the barn and loaded the easels into the van, Joy escorted Cynthia to her studio. Cynthia stepped around the room while Joy remained just inside the door biting the end of her pinky finger. Cynthia slipped the cigarette holder in her pocket. She removed her floppy hat and hung it on a hook. Her hair was short and styled like a flapper girl's. She actually looked like Natalie Wood, Joy thought, in a movie about Zelda Fitzgerald.

Before saying anything about any of the paintings in the room, Cynthia slipped a novel from the bookcase. "You're a reader." She flipped through a soft-cover copy of *Girl With a Pearl Earring*.

"I am." She pointed at the book Cynthia was holding. "I like that one."

"What do you like about it?"

"That it's not quite Cinderella. I don't like stories that work out too neatly in the end."

"I think I must know too much about seventeenth-century art to like a novel about one of the most recognizable paintings from that time."

"Knowing too much can be a hindrance."

Cynthia thought about what Joy said. She held the novel up. "Do you think it's a work of art?"

"The novel or the painting?"

"The novel hasn't been around long enough to know."

Joy didn't agree but decided not to say. "I like Vermeer. There's life in his paintings. But if I had to pick a Renaissance painter it would be Caravaggio."

"Really."

"There's muscle in his work. My favourite is *Judith Beheading Holofernes*."

"Now wouldn't that be a novel to read."

Joy smiled. Cynthia handed her the book and Joy hugged it to her chest.

"I think there's muscle in *your* work." Cynthia turned on her heel, taking in the paintings around the room again.

Joy's heart thumped. "That's very kind of you."

"When I told Mr. Wood he was an artist, that's exactly what he said."

"Really."

"I told him politeness was a weakness. Worse, it's boring. I've only just met you but my impression is that you're neither weak nor boring."

Joy set the book on the small table with the brushes. "Landon's not weak. He's not boring either. He's the reason for all of this."

"I don't think that's true. But it doesn't matter. I can offer you a show at the end of October. Choose your best ten pieces. Write an artist's statement. I'll send Declan in a week with the van. Your work is as good as any I've seen in recent years but buyers and critics can be fickle. So, we shall see."

A show. At *Fuse!*

Joy was busting.

"I'm so." She glanced at the ceiling for the word. Then she looked at Cynthia and smiled. "Pleased."

—◆—

Landon and Joy stood on the porch and watched the white van drive away.

"So. Did she like your paintings?"

Joy folded her arms. "She's giving me a show."

"You mean *you* are giving *her* a show."

Joy considered what she had told Cynthia about Landon. She considered how much she'd been thinking about Harlon. She sighed. "I don't deserve you."

"Deserve's got nothing to do with it."

Landon pocketed his hands and looked at Joy. She tucked her hair and smiled. They were at a point in their relationship where moments and comments like these needed neither explanation nor confirmation.

Joy took one of his hands and opened it. She looked at it. She set her fingertips to his and traced the length of his fingers to his palm, then to his wrist where she stopped and brought the tips of her own fingers together. She matched her fingertips to his again and repeated the tracing down to his wrist. He watched her do it. He hoped she would do it again.

—◆—

Inside her studio Joy opened Molly's journal and read the story. She had read it every day since finding the journal in the basement. She took the title—*Nightsounds*—and gave it to her painting of the wolf. She still thought about Harlon when she looked at the painting. She thought about him when she heard a wolf howl in the distance, which happened most nights. When she paddled the river she fell into daydreams that featured him. Some mornings over coffee she looked at Landon and thought of Harlon. Sometimes when Landon's lips were on her lips, when his lips were on her body, she imagined they were Harlon's lips. Sometimes when Landon was inside her she pretended it was Harlon inside her. She loved Landon. She was certain she did. Maybe it was the thinking about Harlon that made her think about him more. Maybe it was the idea of him she liked. How could she know? Maybe if she saw him again the feelings would stop.

She bit her bottom lip.

Maybe if she saw him again the feelings would be stronger and she would have to do something about it. Like she always had.

She flipped to a blank page in Molly's journal.

Cynthia wanted an artist's statement.

Joy looked around the room at her work.

Okay. Let's see if we can get down on paper what some of all of this means.

Joy, in Molly's journal

A painter creates light, or lack of light, and captures what is not there. A painter paints the way a lover loves. A painter muscles. A painter whispers. A painter touches. A painter feels.

Man At Work. The face doesn't matter. It's the body. The tool in the hands, the hands themselves. The power. The grace. The sweat. The blood in the veins.

(N)ascent. A chrysalis breaking open, the dry spent shell flaking away, the wet wings within beginning to spread, the bright body bursting forth.

Forsaken. A red leaf, the tip of its stem frozen in ice. Wind lifts the body of the leaf from the ice but the ice pins the stem in place and will not let it go. There is a struggle: a simultaneous yearning to escape and a frightening awareness that it cannot. A desire, a need to migrate with the others. To disappear. A longing not to be on display. A life that is no longer a life stuck in a place it was never meant to be.

Ghost. The fading imprint of the leaf in the glass surface of the ice as the ice itself is melting. The suggestion is that the leaf in *Forsaken* finally relents, exhausted from the attempt to escape, like an animal coming to accept its cage. Now in the wake of the actual leaf we see where it fell asleep on the bed of ice, its body's impression in the ice like a fossil. Somewhere between *Forsaken* and *Ghost*, the ice lets go of the stem and a gust of wind chariots the dead leaf away.

For Thee. The verdigris bell. How ancient. The sound of it. Through the years.

The Woodsman. An actual ghost. A mystery.

Nightsounds. The wolf. A dream, a nightmare. Real, imagined. Protection, death. Control, helplessness. Strength, an aching. Hunger.

Landon, not only to himself

Has something happened?

No. Not yet.

Why are you so certain something will?

I can feel it.

What do you mean?

The way she holds onto me sometimes. Like she's trying not to let go.

That's not a bad thing.

The way she looks at me—it's like she sees someone else.

IN THE NIGHT

◆◆◆

"**A**re you nervous?"

"Nervous," Joy said. "No. I don't think so."

It was the late afternoon of Joy's show in the city. They were both in the bathroom, getting ready. Landon was wearing his only pair of dress pants and a white sleeveless undershirt, no socks. Shaving cream covered his face. Joy was wearing a black slip, thighs pressed against the double sink, doing her eyes and lips a few inches from the mirror. Landon set the razor to his cheek and drew it down his face.

"I'd be nervous. If it were me."

"In a way it is you."

Landon tapped the razor against the sink's edge.

Joy capped her lipstick and rubbed her lips together. "The paintings—you're in them."

He drew the razor down his face again. "You mean the ones of the man working."

"Those. The others, too."

"—."

"Not to mention, you made all the easels."

"I don't think people go to art shows to see easels."

He pulled the razor up his neck to his chin.

Joy set both hands on the vanity and stared into the mirror. "How do I look?"

"The way you always look." He tapped the razor on the sink's edge again and looked at her in the mirror. "Beautiful."

She wrapped her fingers around the wrist of the hand that held the razor. She took the razor from him. She turned his whole body so that his back was to the mirror. She set the razor to his neck and drew the blade up to his chin, following its course with her eyes. She tapped the razor against the sink's edge, as he had done, and repeated the routine until the job was finished. She ran the water hot and cleaned the razor and set it on the glass shelf above the faucet. She soaked a soft cloth with the hot water and patted his face with it. She took a glass bottle, wet her palms with the blue liquid, and patted his cheeks and neck with it. She looked into the blue liquid of his eyes. She tucked her hair and traced a finger from his sternum to his belt. She undid the buckle. Pulling the tongue of the belt, she made a leash of it. Obediently he followed. With an open hand she pushed him to the bed and took her pleasure before giving him his.

After, she returned to the bathroom where she redid her lips and leaned into the mirror to attend again to her eyes.

Landon remained on the bed, hands clasped over his chest like a dead man. His eyes were closed and he was nearly sleeping.

"I've been meaning to talk to you about something," she said.

He opened his eyes but did not move.

"I've been thinking," she said. "Maybe we should have a child."

Landon inhaled deeply and held it. He thought of his parents. He thought about the word *family*.

"What do you think?"

He exhaled. "I think. You would make a wonderful mother."

In the mirror Joy set her lips together and grinned.

—◆—

When they left Lowbone the sky was a late afternoon cold October blue. Through the window Joy saw a palette of fall colours. She imagined dipping a brush into the red and orange leaves, the brown and yellow fields. She imagined recreating them on a canvas. The radio, tuned to a folk station: guitar and banjo songs of lost love, forgotten hope, and landscapes of places the singers dreamed of returning to. At the end of the hour's drive, the cityscape grew in the windshield as if it were coming out to meet them.

Dusk now and the sky itself had become thick with the colours of the season. It looked like an Afremov painting, Joy thought, come to life.

"I'm glad you came."

Landon furrowed his brow, focused on the road ahead.

"I know how much you hate the city."

"I don't hate the city. I left the city."

"An important difference."

"Yes."

Joy yawned. She wondered if Harlon had found the note she had written, folded and tied with twine, and placed in his mailbox. She wondered if he would show up. If he did, how would she explain his being there to Landon? *The painting of the wolf was inspired by his wolves*, she would say. *I thought it would be a nice gesture. Didn't I tell you?* She had invited Ghazal, too. Landon had given her the card he took from the café. How was it that the only two people other than Landon she could think to invite to her very first opening—at *Fuse!* of all places—were a barista she had bought coffee from three times and a man she'd talked to only once. There was Rose, but Rose had already told Joy that if she could help it she would never set foot in the city again. Joy hadn't asked why but it was enough to abstain from inviting her to the show.

Joy. You have no roots.

Which is why a child might be nice.

Might be nice is no reason to have a child. The idea of a child is not a child. A child is not a painting.

Joy set her head against the cool passenger door window and looked out. The city. She could get lost in the city.

—◆—

At about the same time that Landon and Joy arrived downtown, Harlon received a call from the Lowbone police station. Two cruisers met him on the highway and the four officers helped him lift the deer into the back of his truck. On the way home Harlon called Bill.

When Harlon arrived home Bill was already there, leaning against his truck, arms folded over his chest in his cable-knit sweater. Harlon nodded and said Bill's name. Bill did the same. Harlon opened the gates and handed Bill a heavy steel bar. Harlon had another for himself. They climbed into the back of the truck and worked the deer to the tailgate. The animal was not quite dead. The heart, however slowly, was still beating. The chest rose and fell, almost unnoticeably. There was the slightest trace of breath, the slightest bead of life in the eyes.

The men did not speak.

The combination of the gate's whining hinges, the rumble of the truck, the headlights, and the smell of the deer summoned the pack from deep within the woods. The men noticed the eyes first, glowing in the dark. They heard hunger in their throats.

Harlon climbed down from the truck bed and pulled himself into the cab. He rolled the window down. Bill followed and closed the gate before climbing into his own truck. Behind them the wolves descended upon the body of the deer. Through their open windows in the dark, both men could hear the ripping, the gnawing, the sucking. As he drove away, Harlon imagined the deer feeling some kind of relief as it drew its last breath and closed its weary eyes.

Up at the house he and Bill didn't say a whole lot. They sat and had a beer and then they had another, and then they had one more. It didn't take much, sometimes, to put a night in in Lowbone.

◆

Having parked a block away from the gallery, Landon and Joy walked towards the address on one of the cards Cynthia had given her, advertising the opening.

Joy put a hand on Landon's chest. He felt it there.

"This is it." Joy looked up and down at the heavy silver door, *Fuse!* stamped in white cursive on the opaque glass. She reached for the silver handle and pulled.

◆

Inside, waiters with slicked back hair and bow ties held platters and moved among the guests. Fingers plucked hors d'oeuvres. Flutes of champagne tinked. As if by design there seemed to be the perfect number of people gathered in small groups. Individuals stood, chins in hand, assessing the paintings hung on the walls and standing in the easels. There was a steady patter, a hum.

Joy noticed Ghazal across the room. Her hair was metallic blue and she wore a matching sequin dress, loose at the waist. Her wrists were heavy with silver bangles and she wore knee-high Doc Martens laced tight around the shins. She smiled when she saw Joy wave but not dramatically. The woman standing with Ghazal took her hand.

Joy reached for Landon's hand and squeezed. She turned to him. He looked good in his suit. She went on her toes and kissed his cheek. Even as she did she caught herself thinking about Harlon. She caught herself looking for him.

In the background, the soft lingering voice of Norah Jones beckoned. Joy sang along. She heard the lyrics as an invitation. The singer was beckoning: *come away with me, in the night.*

Joy let go of Landon's hand and stepped into this pinch-herself wonderland she could not yet believe was real.

—◆—

After Bill left, Harlon fed the woodstove and figured it would last until morning. He poured himself a whisky and sat at the kitchen table. Girl settled at his feet. He looked at the note he'd found in the mailbox, folded in on itself and tied with twine. With his jackknife he cut the twine and opened the note. It might go without saying, he would tell the sender should the opportunity arise, that he was not a man who received many notes.

> *Dear Harlon,*
>
> *We met last spring. You might not remember.*

Of course he remembered. How could he not?

> *Anyway, I have this show in the city.*

With the note there was a card that stated a time and a date and a place. He looked at the card.

> *I hope you can make it. Joy Kalm*

Harlon folded the note and slipped it in his shirt pocket. He looked at his watch. Too late now. Even if he wanted to go. Which he didn't, he told himself. But even if he wanted to.

He drank the whisky and poured another and listened to the wood crack and snap in the stove.

—◆—

Cynthia Vale ushered Joy around the gallery, introducing her to critics and amateur art lovers who had a disposable income and a soft spot for up-and-coming artists. By the end of the night she had sold four paintings. If she was lucky the critics and collectors with real clout might saunter by some time over the next two weeks, unannounced as was often their style, and offer an approving nod or two. If she was really lucky they might buy something and make it known.

As much as Cynthia Vale was interested in the art itself, she was equally interested in establishing the artists she promoted as brands. Joy was billed as "an emerging old-world spiritual-realist inspired at once by the styles of Goya and Millais while paying homage to the haunting Renaissance realism of Caravaggio." Of course, Joy's subject matter shared almost nothing in common with these artists, but the point was to provoke a feeling or a sense the viewer might look for in the work. The broadside Cynthia had designed and circulated around the city in anticipation of the opening (making sure to hit all the right shops and cafés and inboxes) invited art lovers and critics alike to join her in introducing one of the country's brightest emergent stars.

◆

Joy Kalm: Nightsounds

Cynthia had taken the title for the show from the painting of the wolf. A blown-up image of the wolf's eyes flanked Joy's name and the title. Cynthia had one of the broadsides framed and gave it to Joy, something she did for all her first-time artists.

Joy sat at a table with a glass of champagne and a stack of broadsides to sign. Ghazal waited until the line diminished. When she approached the table Joy stood and hugged her like they were old friends.

"Congratulations," Ghazal said. "Sister."

Joy smiled. "I'm so glad you came." She leaned in. "Can you believe this?"

"It's amazing. Really." Ghazal bumped the hip of the woman standing next to her. "This is Jewel. She loves *Infinite Jest*, too." Ghazal kissed the hand she was holding. "And me."

Jewel smiled and offered Joy the hand Ghazal had just kissed.

"I love your work. Especially the one called *Ghost*."

"Jewel's a photographer. She takes pictures of people when they're not looking." Ghazal smiled at Jewel. "I tell her it's creepy. She tells me I don't understand."

This time Jewel took Ghazal's hand and kissed it.

Joy watched them. "Understanding is overrated."

Jewel took a glass from a passing waiter and handed it to Ghazal. She took one for herself. "To not understanding." They all clinked glasses and drank.

The way Jewel and Ghazal kissed each other's hand reminded Joy of how she and Victoria had done the same. When she thought about it she realized she had never kissed Landon's hand and he had never kissed hers. She wondered what something like kissing a hand meant. If anything. If everything.

"So, tell me," Ghazal said. "Where are you getting your coffee now?"

Joy leaned in like she was telling her a secret. "In the country."

"I don't think the country and I would get along."

"I wondered about that, too. But you know, it's quiet, peaceful. Which is nice. A person can get a lot done. Or nothing at all. I do miss the city, though."

Ghazal touched her arm, then hugged her. "Stop by some time. Really."

"I will."

"Don't just say you will."

"I won't. I mean. I will. Stop by."

They hugged again and Joy told Jewel how nice it was to meet her. She thanked them both for coming. She watched them go.

Cynthia appeared beside her from somewhere unseen, stirring a martini. "Well. There she is."

Joy looked at Cynthia. "Thank you. For this."

"Don't thank me, my dear. You're the one with the talent and the brush. I'm merely the one with the gallery and the gall."

Joy liked Cynthia. She could see them being friends. "Can I ask you something?"

"Ask away."

"Do you like what you do?"

"Like," said Cynthia. "I don't know that 'like' has anything to do with it. I'm good at it, which is all that really matters."

"I'd like to think if I wasn't any good at painting I'd still like doing it."

"You wouldn't. Now, where is that darling boy of yours? I want to tell him how many people offered to buy his easels."

Landon was on the far side of the room, standing in front of *The Woodsman*.

Cynthia located him. "Ah, there he is. He's so still I thought he was part of an installation." She sipped her martini. "Listen. I mean this in the best way possible. But he certainly is his own kind of strange, isn't he."

Joy tucked her hair. "I like strange."

"Yes. I know what you mean."

Joy thought maybe that was it. Maybe all this time that's what she'd been looking for. Strange. The unexpected. Something not too comfortable. Something she couldn't quite explain.

◆

Landon stood in front of *The Woodsman*, arms behind his back, staring at the painting. He had not seen it before tonight. Joy had started and finished it in the week after Cynthia offered her the show. He could not look away.

Joy and Cynthia joined him.

"So, Mr. Wood. What do you think of our Joy?"

Landon did not like Cynthia's use of the word *our*.

He continued to stare at the painting. "Joy knows what I think."

Cynthia raised a brow, stirred what was left of her martini.

What Landon said was terser than he had intended. He wasn't feeling exactly like himself, if he was being honest. Whatever it was that he felt had been coming on for a while. He thought maybe he should tell Joy. He also thought maybe he shouldn't.

Keeping his arms behind his back he glanced at the floor and wondered briefly if the floor was hardwood or some kind of human-made material manufactured to appear natural and rustic. He scuffed it with his shoe. It felt real but unless he got down on his knees and felt it with his hands and smelled it, he would not know for certain.

He looked at Cynthia. Then he turned to Joy. Gently, he took her face in his hands. He touched his lips to her forehead, his nose to her hair. He brought his face away from hers and held her shoulders, also gently. He looked at her. "I am so—"

Joy straightened his tie. She brushed his lapel. Her eyes said it was okay, she knew. She knew what he meant. His eyes said he was sorry. They were wet. She thumbed the wetness away.

Landon turned abruptly and held his mouth and stared at the painting.

Cynthia gave the waiter a little wave.

Joy looked at the figure in the painting—the man, the ghost—and thought about the first evening she saw him, all those evenings since, standing on the dock by the cedar wood as the sun went down behind her on the river.

She looked at Cynthia. "Do you believe in ghosts?"

"One cannot traipse around this earth as long as I have without having seen a ghost or two."

The waiter arrived. Cynthia returned her empty glass to the tray and took a fresh martini. Joy passed. The waiter held the tray a little longer for Landon. Landon did not respond. The waiter made a slight bow and took his leave.

"Do you, my dear? Believe in ghosts."

"No. I mean, I never used to."

Landon inhaled abruptly and held it. He exhaled and said, "It doesn't matter."

They both looked at him.

Cynthia. "I didn't take you for a nihilist, Mr. Wood."

"I mean it doesn't matter if you believe in something. It either exists or it doesn't."

"An absolutist then."

He looked at her. "Whatever you want to call it. Listen, I would like to buy this painting."

Cynthia raised a brow again. Joy touched Landon's shoulder. He turned to her.

"I want to buy this painting and hang it in our house." He looked at the canvas. "It's so—"

Cynthia rolled her hand at the wrist. "Alive."

Landon looked at her. "Yes. That's exactly what it is."

The word came to the clean white page in his mind.

He looked at the painting. "I can hear him breathing."

—◆—

It was close to midnight. They were nearly home. They hadn't said much. The car was quiet. The radio stations were all static this time of night in the country. Joy fogged the window with her breath and placed her hand there. The window was cold.

Landon made the turn onto Hart Road, then up their driveway to the house. The truck bumped and sidled along. The headlights revealed the old tire tracks a hundred years of coming and going had set down as a path from the road to the house.

Joy looked at the handprint she had made on the window. Most of the palm remained fogged. She saw a face in profile. Her four fingers were the hair, her thumb the nose. She used her pinky finger to make an eye and a brow, a crescent moon mouth. In her head she called this window-man Wilbur. If she ever met Wilbur in real life they would be great friends. Someone to talk about books with, someone to walk with, someone to confide in. No thoughts of what Wilbur's lips would feel like on her lips would ever enter her mind. She would never imagine touching him. She would never imagine her hand in his hair or on his chest. Her heart would not quicken at the thought of him. She would not imagine his body pressed against hers. She would not think of Wilbur in any of these ways. No matter how hard she tried. No matter how hard she didn't. Wilbur would be nothing like Landon had been. Wilbur would be nothing like Harlon.

—◆—

Landon leaned *The Woodsman* against the wall opposite the armchair he liked to sit in. Joy slipped her shoes off in the kitchen and stood in the doorway to the living room and watched him.

Landon held his hands out in front of himself like a director. "It's the perfect spot to hang him. Don't you think?"

Joy held herself and leaned in the doorway, one bare foot crossed over the other.

"He's a ghost, Landon. You can't hang a ghost. He's already dead."

Landon glanced at her, then returned his attention to the painting.

Joy undid her arms and tucked her hair. "I think I might go for walk."

"—."

"Through the woods."

"—."

"Naked."

"—."

"Did you hear me, Landon?"

He turned and looked at her. Took two strides towards her and grabbed her waist, which made her gasp. He turned her sideways and stepped through the doorway. Went to the drawer by the fridge and opened it. He felt the leather string and smelled the fingers he had felt it with. He touched the key. The metal was cold. He closed the drawer and opened the one next to it. Took a wooden-handled hammer from the drawer and rooted around for the right-sized nail. On his return to the living room he stopped and kissed Joy. Hard and quick.

"Proud," he said. "That was the word I was looking for."

Joy watched him find a stud in the wall with his fist and hammer the nail in when he did. He held the painting, like a prize he'd won, and hung it on the wall.

—◆—

Joy drank a glass of wine in the kitchen while Landon sat in the living room in the chair he liked to sit in, staring at the painting. The house was quiet. Joy finished her wine and took the truck keys from the table. She did not put her shoes on. She padded her way to the door and made sure it didn't snap shut behind her. When the truck started Landon glanced toward the kitchen. It would be difficult to tell by looking at him if he had heard the truck pull away. It would be difficult to tell by looking at him if he had given it a second thought.

—◆—

Joy had not driven in a long time. She tried to remember. Victoria's Mini Cooper along the island coast? Sad Paul's scooter in the rain? Michel's beamer in Marseille that time they snuck off to the countryside? She pretended to be Daisy. He wore a Gatsby suit because she asked him to. On the blanket by the river they drank wine and ate bread and when he started kissing her he quoted Bendrix from *The End of the Affair*. He put the lines he quoted in present tense. His thick, beautiful accent. His thick, beautiful lips. "*I have to touch you with my hands. I have to taste you with my tongue. One can't love and do nothing.*" It was all so ludicrous, but also beautiful and intense. Alongside strange she wanted beautiful, too, and intense.

Now, here she was in Landon's truck, their truck, which used to be Harlon's truck, driving the country roads of Lowbone deep into the night of her first ever gallery opening in the city.

She clicked the radio on. Static. She touched the CD button and clicked through the tracks to the one she wanted and drove, two hands on the wheel, while Leonard Cohen sang about the place near the river, the tea and oranges that came all the way from China. She loved the song but thought Leonard could do better than touching her perfect body with his mind. Touch her really, Leonard. Really touch her. Touch her with the orange. Touch her with the tea. The skin of one, the heat of the other. Touch her with the tip of an impossibly soft leaf tethered by its stem to a branch you hold over her like you're witching for water. Touch her with a stone. A cool smooth time-washed stone you rescue in a single, long-held breath from the riverbed below. Present her with the stone as you emerge, breaching the surface like a creature from a myth. Set the stone between your lips and trace her skin with it. From the ball of her foot, to the arch, to the heel, up the curve of her calf to the soft inside of her thigh, all along the line made by the muscle of her abdomen, to her sternum, to the suprasternal notch, in one single unbroken breath-shadowing line. And when you're there, deposit the stone in the shallow her collarbone makes with her neck as the rest of your river-water-wet body maps itself onto hers. The way she wants you to, the way you ache to. Fuck touching her body with your mind, Leonard. Touch her. Like you mean it. Fuck. And say the word when you do.

◆

If someone had asked Joy why she had written the note to Harlon, why she had folded the note and tied it with twine, why she had then placed the note in his mailbox as though it were one in a series of a long-established correspondence, why she hadn't simply gone to his door and knocked and invited him to the show in person, she would say she liked the act of writing notes. A note reached out. A note made her feel like she was part of a novel. A note was closer to permanent the way speaking could never be. Not that she was looking for permanence. A note was real. Whatever she was doing, alongside strange and beautiful and intense, she was always looking for something real.

—◆—

Landon stared at *The Woodsman* until his eyes hurt and became heavy. He fell asleep there in the chair in the living room. While he slept he dreamed of the figure in the painting. In the dream the figure came to life, standing on a dock, staring at something in the distance, a rifle resting on his shoulder. He levelled the rifle, closed one eye, and took aim at something Landon could not see in the dream. The figure in the painting squeezed the trigger, slowly, and Landon watched, trying to ascertain what the figure in the painting was aiming at. In the dream Landon told himself that if he woke right now and left the house and walked through the cedar wood he might see the man in the painting standing on the dock. He might see the ghost.

Landon woke, gripping the arms of the chair. His eyes still hurt. Wood snapped in the stove in the kitchen. He checked his father's watch. Beyond midnight. He smelled the worn leather band of the watch and closed his eyes. He rose and poured himself a whisky and drank it down. He opened the drawer by the fridge in the kitchen. He pinched the leather string and smelled his fingers. He took the key and a flashlight from another drawer and tromped down the stairs to the basement. He disappeared for a while and then came back to the kitchen and returned the key to the drawer. He either knew or he did not know that Joy was not in the house. He grabbed his jacket from the hook by the door. Standing on the porch he thumbed the flashlight on and made his way to the woods.

◆

Harlon was asleep at the kitchen table, head on his folded arms, whisky glass empty. On the record player, Merle Haggard and The Strangers were going on at a low volume about the good old days. Girl, the dog, was in her own slumber under the table at Harlon's feet.

Joy turned off the Glen Road and stopped the truck under The Wolf Den sign. She waited and thought about driving up to the house. She thought about knocking on his door. What would she say when he answered? *Sorry to call so late, but I wrote a note inviting you to a show in the city, and so, yeah, I noticed you didn't come and I was just wondering why.*

Harlon woke. He rubbed his eyes and went to the window. The dog woke, too, and followed him. Harlon saw the headlights pointing up the driveway. Then he saw them go dark.

Joy exited the truck. She was careful not to slam the door. She made her way to the mailbox in her black dress and bare feet. The ground was cold. She could see her breath. She imagined the wolves somewhere deep in the woods. She pictured the animal she had painted. She imagined the pack lying together, sated and sleeping. A family. In her imagining she saw one of the wolves yawn, slow-blinking, pushing himself to his feet. Then another. Eventually the whole pack, coming to life in the night.

◆

Landon pointed the flashlight towards the entrance of the trail. It cast a wide cone, illuminating the path in front of him. The air was cold, redolent of cedar. Sounds of the night birds rose.

"You have to tell Joy what you found," he said, not quite to himself. "Keeping this particular secret a secret will come to no good."

"That's hard to know for certain."

"Telling her will not make her leave."

"And the corollary. Not telling her will not make her stay."

When Landon emerged from the trail on the other side of the woods he stepped onto the dock and breathed deeply in. He exhaled. He looked up. The moon was full, like someone had punched a hole into a sky-sized sheet of black paper and held the sky-sized sheet of black paper up to a strong and shining light.

Somewhere in the distance a wolf howled at the hole-punched moon.

—◆—

Joy opened Harlon's mailbox. It was empty. He'd seen the note. He'd read it. He'd read the note and then decided, for whatever reason, not to come to the show. Maybe he hated the city. Maybe he had no time for and saw no point in what people called art. Maybe he had no time for her.

Joy returned to the truck and climbed into the cab. Again, she was careful to close the door quietly. As she was about to turn the key she saw movement in the near distance.

Harlon and the dog.

She watched them come, unhurried, toward the truck. She opened the door and stepped out. Her bare feet again on the cold ground. She put a hand on the hood of the truck. Harlon moved towards her and set his own hand on the hood near hers. Their fingers nearly touched. He looked at her. She went on her toes. Close enough now she could smell the whisky on his breath, the sweetness of it. She pushed her thighs against his. Her lips ached. He took his hand from the hood and held the back of her head. She looked at him. His eyes, his lips. Her own lips came close to his. She took a quick breath. As though he meant to follow that breath he kissed her and hiked the hem of her dress to her waist. The spaghetti straps fell from her shoulders. Lifting her was nothing. She felt the cold metal of the truck against her back. Two bodies pressed in the night. Mouths half-open, half-touching. She could taste the whisky on his lips. He pulled himself right through her. She dug her heels into the small of his back. *Fuck*, she whispered. Like an answer somewhere deep in the woods came the howl of a wolf.

They hung onto each other. Their breathing settled. Eventually they parted. Joy slipped the straps of her dress to her shoulders, the hem of her dress to her knees. She stepped away from Harlon, backwards, her bare feet again on the cold ground. Her eyes still on him, she opened the truck door and climbed into the cab.

Harlon lit a cigarette and watched her go. When he returned to the house he poured another whisky and threw it down his throat. Standing in the kitchen he lit a match. He unfolded the note she had written him, set a corner to the flame, and watched it burn.

FAMILY PICTURE

--◆◆◆--

November. Near the end. Shorter days, greyer skies.

Four months since Joy had found Molly's journal. A little more than a month since her first-ever gallery opening. A little more than a month since Harlon. Surreal how certain events could feel so life-altering in the moment, then merely remembered, in fragments, for the rest of a life.

--◆--

The show had been successful. By the end of her two-week run she had sold almost every painting. The reviews had been favourable. Cynthia seemed pleased. Another show, perhaps, in a year or so, after she'd had *some time to work and produce something fresh and new*. That was the expectation. Regardless how successful one show was, the next needed to be fresh and new. Which was redundant. New went without saying. And what did fresh mean if not new? Bright? Clean?

She thought about the word *clean*. She thought about the action. It was something she was doing now. For the first time in her life she made the bed in the morning. She tidied the bathroom before leaving it. Wiped the sink, the faucet, the mirror. She swept, not only the floors out in the open but under furniture, in corners. She vacuumed. She did laundry before she ran out of things to wear. She wiped the counters, even the shelves in the fridge. She caught herself dusting.

She hadn't painted since the show. She hadn't even picked up a brush. Landon didn't know that she wasn't painting, occupied as he was. He still spent his days in the barn, working. On what, Joy didn't know. The level of his secrecy had risen. The level of his quiet, too. They ate together, they went to sleep together. They rose in the morning and had coffee together. They listened in the evenings to music together. But together, somehow, felt separate now. She wished there was something she could do to separate the feeling of separateness from her life forever.

All she did these days, it seemed, was sleep and eat and read and clean. All she did these days, if she were being honest, was think about Harlon.

She thought about Harlon and how she was going to tell Landon.

How she couldn't not tell him.

All her adult life she had never encountered the problem of what to do and how to do it. Relationships had always run their course and she had always been the one to end them. She moved on. She wrote the note, snatched a memento, and walked away. Leaving had never been difficult. But this time was different. This time she felt different. This time what she felt was getting in the way. Everything seemed so complicated and she didn't know what to do.

She thought and she thought and she thought, and she felt. She felt deeply.

She felt, hands splayed on her abdomen, the life growing within.

—◆—

Early December. Snow covered the ground. The season's first.

It was midmorning. Joy had brewed a pot of coffee and poured it into a thermos. She had also baked a tray of biscuits and wrapped two of them, cut and buttered and still warm, in waxed paper. At the back of one of the cupboards she had found an old cookbook she decided must have been Molly's. She flipped through the old pages. The word *biscuits* had appealed to her when she saw it. She liked the look of it. Biscuits. When she looked up the word she found that it came from another word that meant baked twice. She liked that idea and thought it was fitting. Maybe a lot of things were better the second time around.

Standing at the sink in the kitchen she looked out the window. Smoke rose from the chimney stack on the barn roof. Landon had installed a woodstove in the barn which he had turned into his shop. He seemed able to do anything. He was so good, so able. Everything he touched became better. He'd been different lately, but that didn't change how good he was. He deserved better. He deserved the truth.

Joy set the thermos and the biscuits on the bench by the door where she pulled on her black boots, her black down jacket, her black toque, her black woollen mittens. Each item had a slash of rust somewhere on it. Under the black toque her hair was like rust. If she were in a magazine she would have been walking a black Lab with a rust-coloured collar, looking over her shoulder at something beyond the frame as she went. She thought about Jewel taking the picture. She thought about Ghazal watching. She thought about what it might be like to move back to the city and have those two as friends.

She thought about leaving. She thought about where she might go. She saw herself leaving Landon for Harlon. A man she'd only talked to once. A man she hadn't seen since that night against the truck in the darkness under the moon.

A man who might be the father. A man who might want to be.

She didn't know.

How could she?

How could she know what she was going to do?

What. Would. She. Do.

Tell Landon she was pregnant. They'd continue to build a life together. Or leave Landon and Lowbone altogether and go on with her own life, separate and elsewhere, as she had always done. Return to the city. Be a single mother there. An urban artist. Friends with Cynthia, with Ghazal and Jewel. She could see herself in that life. Or stay in Lowbone and leave Landon for Harlon. Tell Harlon she was pregnant. Or not, initially. Or ever. She could end the pregnancy without him knowing. She could end it without anyone knowing. It was up to her. There was no one to tell her what to do.

Joy looked around the kitchen, dressed in her black winter things, cradling the thermos and the biscuits. Cradling, she thought, and the word *family* came to mind. The idea. A warmth rose within her and her shoulders felt like someone was pressing down on them. The idea terrified her. She loved the idea. The idea, she realized, would determine what she'd say to Landon, what she would not. The idea of a family, she told herself, is only an idea. An idea, she knew too well, almost never becomes real in the way it's imagined. Ideas are easily forgotten. Ideas are easily replaced.

She opened the door and stepped into the cold. Crunched through the snow to the barn where Landon was working, where the smoke was rising into the cold December air. She would offer him the coffee and the biscuits she had made. It would seem, to a stranger looking in, like nothing had changed.

—◆—

Landon didn't turn around when Joy entered the barn. So in tune with the rhythm of his working lately, he did not notice her. Careful with the thermos and the biscuits in one hand, Joy opened and closed the door. She watched Landon draw the spokeshave the length of the wood in even slicking strokes.

She set a mittened fist to her mouth and made a sound.

He stopped. He turned.

He looked like a stranger standing there. He looked like the one person in this world who might ever really know her. He looked like a man on the cover of a catalogue that sold woodworking tools. He looked like the man standing next to her in family pictures for the next fifty years. He looked like someone from her past she couldn't remember the name of. He looked like someone she thought she might really love. He looked like a man she was about to leave.

"I didn't hear you come in."

She held the thermos and the biscuits against the front of her jacket. "I didn't want to disturb you."

"That's not possible. You can't disturb me."

She looked down at her boots. The snow was melting, spreading, darkening the concrete floor around her like watercolour blooming on paper.

"I didn't think it would be this warm in here."

Landon tapped the spokeshave in his palm. It made a faint smacking sound. He used the spokeshave to point to the far corner. His eyes stayed on Joy. "The woodstove."

"It's nice."

Lips closed, Joy smiled and stepped closer to the table where Landon had been working. She set the thermos and the biscuits down. She took her mittens off and set them beside the thermos.

"It's beautiful," she said, touching the paddle clamped in place.

Landon assessed the spokeshave in his hand. He thought about adjusting the blade. He thought about sharpening it.

She kept her hand on the paddle and looked at him. "You can paddle the river with me in the spring."

Even as she said the words *with me*, she heard the words *without me*. Even as she said the word *spring* the idea seemed so far away it felt like some kind of magical place in a fairy tale only a child could find.

"The store in the city wanted some paddles." He gestured at the others standing in the corner. "I don't have to think much. Gives me something to do."

"Maybe you could make me a paddle for every day of the week." She touched his forearm. "They would all be such beautiful paddles."

Landon remembered how she had put on the hat she found in the front closet the first time they came to look at the house. "I could. If you wanted me to."

She undid her coat. Pulled off her toque and set it down. She picked up the thermos and looked at it. "Do you like coffee?"

"I do."

"A lot of people say they like it. A lot of people drink it and pretend to like it. Even though all they really like is the smell or the effect or the ritual. Or some combination of the three."

He set the spokeshave down and reached for her waist. They had not been this close in a while. When she felt his hands on her she closed her eyes and although she didn't mean to, although she tried *not* to, she thought of Harlon.

She opened her eyes. She kissed him. "Let's do this again."

In the morning, she knew, she would be gone.

CREATURE

—◆◆◆—

Landon woke to a note on Joy's pillow. When he saw the note he closed his eyes and rolled away. He fell asleep again and woke an hour later. He lay there on his side, eyes open, watching the snow through the window. The flakes were big and slow and soft. The room—and everything beyond the room, the whole world—was perfectly silent. If he moved he would ruin it.

Eventually he sat up and smacked his bare feet on the wood floor for the sound. He stood and pulled on his jeans, a sweatshirt over his head. He sat again and pulled on his work socks. He held the bedpost as he walked around it. When he reached for the door he thought maybe she'd be standing on the other side. He thought maybe she'd be in the kitchen. He thought maybe the note was a prelude to some gift she wanted to give him. He thought maybe the note was a clue in some game she wanted him to play. He thought maybe. He thought if only.

When he opened the door it creaked and no one stood on the other side. When he padded out to the kitchen, no one was sitting at the table. The coffee pot was empty and cold. When he crouched to open the woodstove door he saw that all the wood had burned in the night. If he stirred the ashes he might find a few embers, and he might not. He stood and considered the record player on the table in the corner. The arm was up and no music was coming from it.

So.

He started a fire. He brewed a pot of coffee. He cut two thick slices of bread and put them in the toaster. When it popped he slathered the toast with butter. He took an album from the first shelf and put it on: The Byrds, *Fifth Dimension*. He sat and drank his coffee and ate his buttered toast and listened to the music while the note Joy left him sat on her pillow, beckoning.

What would happen if he left it there and slept beside it every night? What would happen if he took it like a dead thing and buried it? What would happen if he set it in the garden and let the snow cover it? What would happen to it in the spring? Would it break apart? Would a daisy push through the centre of it? Would an animal take it and put it in its nest? Would it disintegrate? Would it turn to earth? What would happen if he tore up the note into a thousand tiny pieces without ever reading what it said and then threw all the pieces in the air like confetti? What would happen if he opened the woodstove door and tossed the note in and watched it burst into a flame he could set his hands to and warm them against?

Staring across the table where Joy sat every morning— where she had sat only yesterday—Landon said, out loud to the empty room, "What would happen?"

He sat that there, staring, sipping his coffee, listening to David Crosby wonder with him. *Who do you think you are? What are you doing here? What's going on? How is it supposed to be?*

Earlier, as the sun was beginning to pull itself into the morning sky, Joy had dressed in her matching black winter things. She had taken her canvas pack stuffed with a few clothes and Molly's journal. She had set the note on her pillow. She had left. As she had always done. As she would more than likely do again.

It was cold and snowing. She slung the pack over a shoulder and hugged herself the whole way to Harlon's. It wasn't far but it felt far. It felt like she'd walked all night. When she ascended the porch steps they felt like the same porch steps she'd descended less than an hour before. The door looked like the same door she had closed quietly behind her. Her black toque and her black coat and her black mittens were white with snow. She stood there and wondered what she was doing.

She heard the opening line of Tenille Townes's song "Where You Are" and sang softly along. She'd been high, too. She'd been low. She'd been everywhere a soul can go.

When she finally knocked, her mitten softened the sound, so she took the mitten off and knocked again.

She heard the legs of a chair scrape the kitchen floor within. She heard his sock-footed steps. She saw the handle turn. She watched the door open. She smiled. She felt like a complete stranger. She felt like she was coming home.

—◆—

Landon sat on the edge of Joy's side of the bed. He sensed the note beside him. Like a creature staring at him. Without looking he reached for it. The paper felt thick. He set the note in his lap and pulled both ends of the twine. The loops of the bow disappeared. The twine lay limp in his lap. He unfolded the paper. The wooden ring he'd made her was inside. He read the note:

I tried. I'm sorry. I love you. Goodbye.

—◆—

Harlon stood there with the door open and looked at Joy in her black coat and boots and toque, covered in the snow coming down. She tried to read his eyes. Her heart thumped hard. It was this feeling, this feeling that she loved.

Harlon didn't say a word and neither did she. Stepping out of the way he clutched the door with one hand and held the other out towards the kitchen behind him, as if he was introducing her to someone who wasn't there.

Her breath-cloud in the cold was like a speech bubble with no words.

She stepped into the house and let the pack slip from her shoulder. She turned to him. He closed the door.

—◆—

Landon stood from the bed. He put the ring in his pocket. The note fell to the floor. He left it there like evidence. He folded his arms and touched his lips with a finger. He thought about biting the nail, hard. He went to the window and looked out. He returned to Joy's side of the bed and looked at the pillow. He could see the impression her head had made in the night. In his mind he saw her lying there. Eyes closed, lips parted. The colour of her hair, the colour of aged wood. Like the bed they slept in. The table in the kitchen where they ate. The chairs they sat on. The paddle he carved from the length of cherry he'd found on the middle shelf against the back wall of the basement. Where he'd found the hammock. The key in the old tobacco tin. The crack in the wall behind the shelf that turned out to be the seam of a secret door.

He wanted Joy. He wanted her there.

He closed his eyes.

When he opened them the bed was still empty. He stood in that spot for a long time and stared at the empty bed. He stood there and stared and stared and stared. He picked up Joy's pillow and looked at. He looked at it like someone deciding whether they wanted to buy it, like someone deciding whether they should throw it away. He stared at the pillow in his hands and then he buried his face in it. He breathed in through his nose and held the breath that held her smell like smoke in his lungs and he did not want to let it go.

Eventually, he took the pillow from his face and looked at it again. He looked at it and he did not know what to do. Like someone lost in the woods, scared for his life. He drove his face into the muted softness of the pillow again and as hard as he could he screamed.

—◆—

Joy moved around Harlon's kitchen like it was a cave she had discovered, trailing a finger along the tops of the chairs, the table, the counter. She couldn't believe how similar it was to the kitchen she had just left. She walked over to the record player in the corner. The song was just ending. She lifted the arm and let the record spin. She covered her mouth to stifle a laugh. How would she explain laughing? How would she explain any of this?

She turned on a heel and stepped towards Harlon. He watched her. Like a fixture, he didn't move. His arms were crossed. She undid them like a bow. He let her.

"I have an idea," she said. "Let's not say anything."

She tried to remember if there was any dialogue in the Garden of Eden story. She didn't think so. Without speaking they had been okay. They had been better than okay. Until the snake arrived. A snake arrives in every garden story. Joy had been the snake herself in her share of garden stories. When she hadn't been the snake, she had often been the one who invited it in. Sometimes she wore the snake like a scarf to show how unafraid she was.

Maybe she could live in some kind of pseudo garden paradise with this man she couldn't stop thinking about. If only for a little while. Maybe if she told this man he was the father of the child growing inside her they could have a life together. Maybe she could fence this garden in. Maybe she could kill the snake this time when it tried to slither past the gate. She could flay the snake and they could cook it over a fire. They could pick the fruit from the branches of the tree they ate under and let the juices run down their chins. They could lie down under the tree in this garden together and feel the roots pulling their way deep down into the ground beneath them.

Harlon plucked the toque from Joy's head and let it drop to the floor. She tucked her hair. They looked at each other.

"You are a strange and beautiful creature," he said.

She looked at his mouth and set a shushing finger to his lips.

IN THE DEEPEST PART

—◆◆◆—

Winter came to Lowbone. There was more dark than there was light and more quiet than there was not. Landon was alone but it wasn't the alone part he was having difficulty with. It was the specifically being without Joy part. He had stopped working. He spent a lot of time in the living room, staring at *The Woodsman*. He spent a lot of time in the basement. He didn't eat much. One bottle of Valpolicella sat on the kitchen counter in the wine rack he had made. He did not open this bottle. He would only open it when Joy returned, which he believed she would. More than believed. Belief alone was for the impractical and the desperate, and Landon was neither impractical nor desperate. He knew she would return. In the deepest part of his bones, he felt it.

Landon, not only to himself

You need to do something.

Like what.

Look for her.

She's not lost. She's gone.

You could find out where.

How?

Ask around.

Then what?

You could read her books.

What good would that do?

It would be better than what you're doing.

Maybe.

Remember what it felt like when she read to you?

Yes.

If you read her books, you would hear the words in her voice.

That would be nice.

It would be like she was right there with you.

Not really.

It can't hurt.

There's always the potential to hurt.

There was almost nothing to do around the sanctuary in the winter. It was closed to visitors and the wolves subsisted on their own. Harlon believed making them fend for themselves through the winter helped keep them wild. He believed it helped keep them wolves.

What helped keep Harlon and Joy who they were were their habits. Harlon woke early. He drank coffee and listened to records. When the paper came he read it. For dinner they either ordered in or ate at The Heather. Joy slept late. Joy went to the bookstore. She bought new books. She talked to Rose. Although Rose knew about Joy's new arrangement she didn't say anything about it. What they did talk about were the books Joy bought and the characters that inhabited them. It always sounded like Rose was talking about people she knew. At Harlon's, Joy used the spare room as a studio. She ordered paint and canvases and brushes. She started to paint again.

Harlon drank beer in the evenings, sometimes whisky, and he never asked why Joy did not. She talked about the books she read and the paintings she was working on. He listened. He never asked about Landon. He never asked about her past and she never asked about his. Sometimes she thought about Landon. Sometimes she wrote about him in Molly's journal. Sometimes she thought about Molly. She wondered if Harlon knew what had happened. She wondered if he knew she was pregnant and wasn't saying. She should tell him soon. She had to know if his knowing would change things. She had to know what his knowing would do.

Joy, in Molly's journal

We say love resides in the heart because we need to give it a home. Because we cannot let love wander. Even though we wander ourselves. As long as we take our hearts with us, we can wander anywhere. At heart, I am a wanderer.

If I could travel back in time I would live among the Bedouin in the Jordan River Valley and learn to gather water from under stones and eat goat cooked over open fires. I would learn their poetry and sing it to their sky gods. I would ask them to tattoo my face with smoke. I would learn how they dance. I would summon lovers with the movement of my eyes and my lips and my feet on hot sand. I would let them take me in, knowing in the deepest part of the heart I wander with that one morning I would wake and want something new, knowing full well that I could not tell them to their beautiful brown faces, those who came to welcome and love a stranger, that I was leaving, that a true drifter never remained anywhere or with anyone except in her own heart. I would find some kind of skin, stretched and dried, to write on. I would find a jar of ink and a sharpened bone to write with. I would learn, some time before I left, how to write *I tried* in Arabic. *I'm sorry. I love you. Goodbye.*

NEW BEGINNINGS

––◆◆◆––

December 31st.

Harlon and Joy were in the living room. He sat forward in his chair opening a wooden box he had set on the coffee table. The box looked old. It looked like the box Joy had dreamed about and found in the basement of The Hart Farm.

She folded her hands together and set them on her knees which were touching. "I've been meaning to ask you something."

Sifting through the contents of the box, Harlon glanced at her.

"Did you ever know Robert and Molly Hart?"

"What would make you ask that?"

She shrugged. He didn't see her.

"I don't know. I was curious."

He placed the items he took from the box on the table: what looked to Joy like two wooden bookmarks, a little glass jar filled with lead-coloured beads, two spools of translucent thread, pliers, scissors, a wooden-handled knife with a long thin blade that looked like it could pierce a heart with no effort at all.

"What's all this?"

"All what?"

"This." She waved a hand over the table. She picked up one of the wooden bookmarks and tapped her palm with it, then Harlon's forearm. She grinned. "Is this to spank me?"

"It's a tip-up."

He took it carefully from her and set it down.

She picked up the glass jar and shook it. The little beads rattled inside. "What are these?"

He looked at her. "Split-shots."

"Tip-up," she said, enunciating the syllables like it was a word from another language. "Split-shots."

"You've never been ice fishing."

"I went salmon fishing once. On the ocean."

Harlon nodded. He had never seen the ocean.

Joy slapped her hands together. "I'm hungry."

Harlon sat back in his chair. He checked his watch. "It's two-thirty."

She reached a hand and trilled her fingers. He looked at her fingers. He sighed but not defeatedly and reached for the hand reaching for him. Joy had a way, and Harlon, one among the many, could not help but love the way she had.

—◆—

On the last day of the year Landon sat at the kitchen table listening to The Civil Wars sing "I Had Me A Girl," and made two lists.

Things To Do

ask around: the train station, the bus depot
read her books
sleep in the bed

Things About Joy I Love

the way she speaks
her eyes, her lips, her art
how she sleeps, how she wakes

how she tucks her hair, how she wrinkles her nose
how she walks with her hands in her back pockets
how I could hold her with one arm against me, forever

—◆—

Harlon leaned on the counter and waited for their drinks. He
didn't have to order them. They were the same every time: beer
for him, root beer in a glass bottle for Joy, with a straw. He
nodded when the drinks came and took them to the table by the
window where Joy was already sitting. Harlon sat and finished
half his beer in one go.

Esther came to their table with her notepad. "What'll it be
for the two lovebirds today?"

Joy watched Harlon down the second half of his beer. "Fish
and chips for me. And it looks like another round for Mr. Glen."

Esther jotted Joy's order and considered Harlon for a
moment. "Bit of an early start."

Harlon wiped his mouth with his forearm. A grin on his
face. "You're not judging me now, are you, Esther?"

"No judging. Only noticing."

"Well." He held the empty glass in the air. "We've lots to
celebrate."

Esther looked at Joy. Joy tucked her hair and shook her
head, very slightly. She reached across the table and took one
of Harlon's hands. "Yes. We do." She looked at Esther. "It's New
Year's Eve." She made the next bit sound far more significant
than it was. "And in two days, it will be a month."

"What will be a month?" Harlon said.

Esther looked at Joy and raised her brow. "Nothing gets by
this one." She spoke to Harlon. "Now. What're you going to eat?
You can't just sit here and drink beer all day."

"Well. I could. But you'd better bring me a burger and fries
to soak her up with. Maybe some pretzels. Keep me thirsty."

"Never known you not to be thirsty."

Esther left and Harlon leaned back in his chair. He grinned and looked at Joy. He didn't know if he loved her yet, but god damn it if he didn't love being with her. Whatever that sonofabitch from the city'd done to drive her away Harlon was the more fortunate man for it.

Esther brought their food and another beer for Harlon. He raised his glass and drank and sucked his top lip when he finished. Joy sipped the root beer through the straw and watched him. It was just after three in the afternoon. She slipped a hand below the table and pressed the palm against her shirt just above her belt. Part of what she loved, she realized, about the things in her life that she loved, was the uncertainty.

—◆—

Landon stood at the bedroom door and opened it. He hadn't slept in the bed in weeks. Tonight he would. Tonight he would check sleeping in the bed off his list. He stepped into the room and took Joy's pillow in his hands. He looked at it. He replaced it next to his and walked around to his side of the bed. He pulled the sheets up and flattened them with an open hand. He fluffed his own pillow and set it down. He stood there and assessed his work. Took the lists from his back pocket and looked at them. Put the one that named the things he loved about Joy in the drawer of the bedside table. A pair of pinecones rustled quietly as he slid the drawer shut. He wondered, did buses and trains run on holidays? Would a wicket be open?

The word *wicket* reminded him of when he told Joy about the *Twilight Zone* episode. He pictured them both in The Pinecone Café sitting in the chairs by the fireplace. The painting of the barn. The coop. The god in the sky. He could hear the music that was playing when they left. He remembered how people had reacted to Joy as she walked out of the coffee shop singing. He could hear her voice. He could hear the words. The bit about wandering around the darkened land all night. He remembered what he'd said to her but meant only to think. *I want to know everything there is to know about you.* How she told him all he had to do was ask.

He looked at the list in his hand. He slid it back into his pocket. Clutching the bedpost, he pulled himself towards the door. Her studio. He remembered seeing her journal there.

"All you have to do is ask," he said to the empty room, in a voice not quite his own.

—◆—

It was getting late. Joy told Harlon she wanted to go and he held a single finger in the air.

"One more. One more."

Joy closed her eyes. When she opened them Bill was setting two fresh pints on the table.

"So tell me," he said. "What ever happened the city boy?"

Harlon took up his beer. "Hell you want to know about him for."

Bill shrugged. "Curious."

"Always thought he was a bit fuck'n strange myself."

Joy folded her arms. "You met him once."

"Twice. But who's counting."

Bill. "Sorry. Didn't mean to hit a nerve."

Joy. "Don't be sorry. I'm fine."

Harlon sat up. "She ain't wrong there. She is fine."

Joy turned to Bill. "I remember you weren't very nice to him."

"I should be sorry about that. But I did not like him. From the get-go."

Joy wanted to ask him why, but it was late and she was tired and she wanted to go.

She looked at Harlon. He sipped his beer. His eyes were almost shut.

"I think I'd better get Mr. Glen home," she said.

"You can't go home. It's almost the New Year."

"Look at him. He's a mess. He wouldn't know a New Year from the end of time."

Harlon hadn't been listening. Focused on his beer, he set the glass down on the table like it was something he feared he might break.

"You know."

The other two looked at him.

He picked his glass up and took another slow drink and then set the glass carefully down again. "I think you might still love'm."

"You're drunk. Where are the keys?"

Harlon closed his eyes and showed Joy one hand like a crossing guard. "You're right. I am. Drunk." He pulled the keys from his pocket and dangled them in front of his face. He dropped the keys on the table and Joy took them. He took another slow drink of his beer and smacked his lips. "But I have one more question." He pointed at Joy even though he wasn't really looking at her. "For you."

Harlon hadn't asked any questions but Joy kept the observation to herself. She was about to stand and go.

"Why," he said, screwing a finger in the air, "don't you ever drink with me? I saw you drink with him."

By *him* Harlon meant Landon and by *drink with* he could only mean the one whisky she'd had the night she and Landon had come to see the wolves feed. Harlon didn't know about all the evenings Joy spent with Landon on their porch with their records and wine. He didn't know anything about them at all. Until now he had taken to heart what she said to him the morning she showed up at his door. *Let's not say anything.* He hadn't needed her to explain what she meant. *Let's not say anything* meant let's not say anything about our pasts. *Let's not say anything* meant let's not say anything about her leaving Landon. It meant let's not say anything about Landon period. It meant let's not ask any questions at all. Let's not complicate things. Let's let this thing between us be what it is and not call it anything.

But Harlon was drunk and Bill had stirred things up a bit already. So what the hell. He was breaking the rule. He was not not saying anything.

Esther had stopped to clear the table of empty glasses.

"She's pregnant, you moron."

Esther took Harlon's not-quite-empty glass from him and dropped it on the tray with the others.

It had been a long night for Esther. She hated New Year's Eve and she was tired and she was sick of people.

Joy's eyes widened. Earlier—it felt like another day entirely—Esther had understood with a simple look that Joy had not told Harlon yet. Now, hours later and at the end of her own tether, Esther blurted it out like it was anyone's news to tell. What Joy felt surprised her. What she felt was relief.

Bill stood and pulled Harlon up with him. Bill held his glass high in the air and called out to everyone in The Heather. "Next round's on Harlon. Fucker's gonna be an old man."

Cheers went up everywhere and Bill downed his beer. He set the glass carefully on Esther's tray and she gave him a look to beat hell.

"Ah, now, come on, Esther. Don't look so miserable. You know you love me."

Bill laughed and threw his arm around Harlon and ushered his friend to the bar and they ordered another round.

Joy pushed her chair away from the table, stood, and touched Esther's arm. "Thank you."

"I don't know what happened with the one you come here with last spring. But he seemed decent to me. A little odd but decent." She threw her chin at the bar. "You've your work cut out with that one."

Joy looked towards the bar and thought about what Esther said. She watched Harlon and Bill clink glasses and drink. She thought about Landon. She wondered if he was okay.

◆

Landon opened the door to Joy's studio and looked inside. The room was dark and still and quiet. He flicked on the light. A blank canvas stood on the easel in the middle of the room. The brushes stood in a jar on a small table. Her apron hung by the door. Her books leaned unevenly and lay stacked on the shelves of the bookcase. The tin bucket she had painted a daisy on stood on the windowsill with her matching yellow rubber boots. Landon went to the bookcase. He picked up the little canoe he had carved her and thought of the life-sized one he had made her. He pictured her in the boat, paddling the evening river. He thought of the last thing she had said to him before she left. *Let's do this again.* He replaced the canoe on the shelf and scanned the titles. He thought of the story Joy had read him in the library. He remembered liking it. He remembered the image of the fish. He remembered the man lying on the ground. He took a thin volume from the shelf and flipped through it. He closed it and looked at the cover. He liked the sound of the title. The picture on the front was a painting of a house and an old truck by the sea. He turned the book in his hands. He opened it and pressed his nose to the pages. He liked the smell and so he did it again. He took the book. He found Joy's journal and took it, too. He closed the door behind him when he left. He went to the living room and sat in the chair he liked to sit in. He looked at the painting on the wall. He flipped through the journal and decided to save reading it. Then he opened the book and started to read.

---◆---

New Year's Day. 5:30 a.m.

Joy woke to the smell of coffee and toast and bacon. Before opening her eyes she felt for Harlon beside her in the bed and found he wasn't there. She put the fingers of both hands against her eyes like a cloth and, with a deep yawn, wiped the night away. She sat up, tucked her hair, and made her way to the kitchen.

Harlon was crouched in front of the woodstove, stoking the fire. He sensed her standing in the doorway behind him. He closed the woodstove door and replaced the poker in its stand. He stood and turned.

"Coffee?"

"I don't think I'm supposed to." She glanced at the floor. She looked at him. She shrugged. "But sure. What can it hurt?"

Harlon poured them both a cup and they sat at the table.

She sipped the coffee and closed her eyes. It was good.

He looked at the spot on the table directly in front of her like he was trying to see through the wood. "How are you—you know—feeling?"

"All right. I think. Okay."

He sat back in his chair. "Listen. I, uh."

"It's a lot to digest. You don't have to say anything."

Harlon looked over his shoulder to the sound of the toast popping. He asked Joy if she was hungry. She said she wasn't. He went to the counter, buttered the toast, and made a sandwich of the bacon he had cooked. He sucked his fingertips clean, pressed the sandwich flat, and cut it in two. Joy watched him. She was here now. This is where she was.

Harlon returned to the table with his sandwich and the coffee pot. He topped up his cup and set the pot down. He sat and bit the sandwich. As he chewed he closed his eyes. He swallowed and let out a sound of pleasure and relief.

"I thought you might be dead."

Harlon took another bite and gave a little laugh. "It was a good night."

Good, she thought, was not the word. She looked at the sandwich in his hands. "I don't know how you're eating that."

"Old country cure." He took another bite.

Harlon checked his watch and continued to eat.

"I understand if it's too much. I should've told you sooner. I should've told you the morning I showed up here."

He swallowed. "I just don't know how I didn't know."

"Some women don't show until very late. Some barely at all. I guess I'm one."

Harlon set a hand on the table. "Whatever happens. I want to—you know—be there."

Joy understood that this was as close to a commitment that Harlon could make.

He checked his watch again and glanced over his shoulder at the door.

"Expecting someone?"

He looked at her. "Sorry. No."

"Going somewhere then."

He nodded. "Fishing. Season opens today. Bill and me always go." He pushed himself from the table and stretched his hands high over his head like some kind of victory gesture and he made the sounds that went with such stretching. Then he rubbed his hands together and smiled. "I'll catch you a big one."

She pressed her lips together and tried to smile. "How do you wish a fisherman good luck?"

"Tight lines."

She stood from the table and padded over to him in her sock feet. She took his face in her hands. She looked *in* and *around* and *at* his eyes. "Tight lines, Harlon Glen. Don't let the big one get away."

———◆———

Landon sat in the living room and read. He read for a long time. He wanted to tell Joy. He wanted to tell her if they had music and this place and each other and their work and now books—he wanted to tell her: now that they had books—then what else did they need? What else could they possibly want?

But Joy wasn't here. Joy was gone. Landon was alone and he felt it.

He looked at the cover of the book in his hands. *The Lost Salt Gift of Blood*. The truck reminded him of his truck. The house reminded him of this house. The smoke rising from the chimney announced the people within. Real people with real lives and all the heartache and happiness that went with real people and real lives.

He opened the book and started reading the first story again. The second sentence stopped him: *"It will be a long winter and I will be alone here."* The coincidence was almost too much. The story's violent final scene stayed with him. He flipped to the title story, which was about a man who gets a letter telling him he is a father, and so he jumps in his car and drives a thousand miles to meet for the first time the son he did not know he had. The boy, ten, lived with his maternal grandparents in a village near the sea. The boy's mother lived far away in another province in a city. She died in a car accident and the grandparents thought the man should know. When the man, at the end of his journey, quite literally comes to the end of the road, he finds the boy fishing in the harbour. The boy doesn't know who the man is. By the end of the story, even though it's clear the man wants nothing more than to take his son with him, home to the Midwest, he realizes the boy is where the boy is meant to be. The boy is already loved. The boy already has a family. The boy is already home. The story made Landon think of his own parents. It made him think of what Joy had said the night of her opening before they left for the city.

Landon sighed. He stood and went to the studio to return the book to its spot on the shelf. He had taken the time to organize the books by title. He chose another one to read.

One day Joy will come home, he thought. She will. One day she will.

The word *will* appeared on the clean white page in his mind.

He thought of all the meanings.

The future.

Certainty.

Possibility.

Determined to do.

An ability to decide.

To make something happen.

What we leave behind.

Joy, in Molly's journal

What are you going to do, Joy, leave again in the night? Write your cryptic little note? Fold and tie it as if the way a note like that looks matters at all?

You have to stop disappearing. It's not just you anymore.

Roots are taking hold.

Roots are taking hold whether you want them to or not.

Landon, not only to himself

It sounds to me like you have managed to keep what happens in your life within your control for a long time.

For a long time. Yes.

You won't want to hear this, but Joy has taken that from you.

I know.

You should tell someone what you found here.

I don't want to tell anyone.

You can't keep this a secret forever.

Why not? Everyone keeps secrets. As for forever, there's no such thing.

A SMUDGE OF BLUE PAINT, LIKE A BRUISE, ON HER SHOULDER

—◆◆◆—

Four months later, a year to the day since he had left the city with Joy—after having spent a long, quiet winter alone on the farm—Landon drove into town. He parked and walked down Main Street and stood in front of the Lowbone Arms & Gallery. He breathed in and held it. He opened the door and walked in. It was the first time in his life he had ever been in the same room as a firearm. The feeling of being in the shop was opposite to the one he expected. He liked the smell of the oil and the metal. He liked the library-level quiet.

The man behind the counter placed his hands flat on the glass display. He had a long beard and was mostly bald. The shirt he wore advertised the store with what looked like a target in the middle of the shirt and two rifles crossed like an X.

Landon stepped to the counter. "I have recently purchased two hens and built them a coop. I want to protect them. I've seen predators lurking at dawn."

The man stepped from behind the counter and stood in front of the wall of rifles. A finger to his lips, he assessed the selection he knew intimately.

Landon stood beside the man and watched him thinking.

The man took a gun from the wall. He cradled the weapon by the butt and the barrel, held it like an offering for Landon to take.

"Here. See how she feels."

Landon looked at the man, then the gun, then the man. "She won't bite. I assure you."

Landon didn't think much of assurances these days but he took the gun in his hands nonetheless. The weight and the cold of it surprised him. At first he held it the way the childless hold infants when friends thrust newborns upon them: rigidly, worriedly, with the threat of something about to go terribly wrong.

The man took the rifle from Landon and showed him how to hold and cock it. Then he gave it back to Landon and Landon followed the lesson. With the butt nestled into his shoulder he cradled the long barrel with his left hand while the fingers of his right found the lever action. Closing an eye, he cocked the lever and sighted a bull's eye on the wall by the door. The feel and the sound of the lever clicking pleased him.

"She looks good on you," the man said. "Natural."

Landon set the butt on the floor and clutched the barrel near the top by the sight. He hipped his other hand. If someone were to snap a picture of him in this moment and run the image through a sepia filter it would look like one of those staged portraits from a hundred years ago.

"I'll take it," Landon said. "And whatever I need to make it fire."

＋

At home, Landon loaded the rifle with a cartridge the way the man had shown him. The sun sat in the sky, restful, like it meant never to leave. A spring breeze lifted and swirled and moved the newly budded branches of the old trees that lined the property. Landon lifted the rifle into position, closed an eye, and sighted a bird on a branch in the distance. A sparrow. When he squeezed the trigger the butt kicked against his shoulder the way he expected and he was able to control it. The sparrow never saw it coming. The bullet exploded its body. A puff of feather and flesh and bone. In the aftermath there was little evidence that the bird ever was.

—◆—

Landon went to the stone well and pumped a cupful of clean, cold water. Resting the gun against the well he stood there, one hand on his hip, and drank the water. He looked up at the sky. He breathed in and held it. He felt good. *Good* was the word. He had not felt this good in a long time.

He went into the house and stood the rifle by the back door. Joy would disapprove. But Joy was no longer here. He pocketed his hands and looked at the gun. He liked the way it looked standing there.

He went to the drawer beside the fridge and opened it. He hung the key around his neck, then padded down the stairs to the basement and went to the shelves against the back wall where he had discovered the secret he meant never to tell anyone.

Not long after he had found the hammock and the key last spring, he had returned to the basement for one of the tobacco tins filled with nails. When he pointed the flashlight at the top shelf he saw what looked like a crack in the wall behind the shelves. He touched the crack and followed it with his finger, expecting it to meander like a river down the wall. Soon he realized it was not a crack but a seam outlining a door. He set the flashlight down and moved the shelves. He clutched the casket-like handle he found recessed in the wall and pulled but the door was locked. He brushed the dust away from below the handle, like an archeologist, and felt the keyhole with his thumb. He left the basement and went upstairs and opened the drawer by the fridge. He took the key on the leather string and returned to the basement. When he slipped the key in and turned it, the mechanisms of locking let go. He pulled the handle again and there was an echo. He took a deep breath and held it. He opened the door and shone the light within.

Landon, not only to himself

Did you buy the gun?

I did. I can protect the chickens now.

You might find you need to protect more than the chickens.

I thought about that.

You'll need to practise.

I thought about that, too. I tried it out when I got home. I managed to shoot a bird from some distance. A sparrow.

How did it feel?

I didn't feel anything. I found it wasn't a very difficult thing to do at all.

Joy, in Molly's journal

All those different skies and one sun. One moon.

My heart in the hands of the ones I love.

My love in the heart of the one inside.

Joy stood in the doorway between the kitchen and the living room while Harlon lay on the floor buried in the cupboard beneath the sink. Joy was wearing an old pair of jeans, a red-and-white plaid patch on one thigh, a sun-yellow tank top, and matching slip-on shoes. She stood there in the doorway and held her taut belly—protective, proud, curious—the way a child might hold a helium balloon: squeezing slightly, careful of the pressure, worried it might pop, nervous to let go.

Harlon—his worn leather work boots planted flat on the floor—reached up under the sink with the rattle and clank and grunt of his fixing. He looked, Joy thought, like a creature from a myth. The taps were his eyes. The faucet, his nose. The sink, his ever-wide mouth. Like a Kafka bug, partially squished, the little legs alive and working.

She watched him and then she spoke. "I'm hungry."

He couldn't hear her for the clanking.

She waited for a pause in the noise and then she tried again. She said his name.

He dropped the heavy wrench, pulled his body and his head clear from under the sink, and sat up on the kitchen floor. His eyes found hers.

She put her hands on the small of her back and pushed her hips forward, stretching, and she glanced at the clock on the wall. His eyes followed hers.

He looked at her and nodded, then pushed himself from the floor and wiped his forehead. He wiped his hands on his pants and walked over to her. He placed his hands on her belly and looked at them there.

She looked down at his hands and felt a kick. Harlon pulled his hands away like he'd felt an electric shock and his eyes widened.

"Looks like somebody else is hungry, too," Joy said.

Harlon smiled and took her hand. Slid his thumb between her fourth and pinky finger, where she used to wear the wooden ring Landon had made her. She felt safe. She felt a longing. She felt betrayal. She felt love.

Joy and Harlon left the house and walked to The Heather. Joy looked up and saw one cloud move in front of the sun. She took note. She would paint that cloud. She would paint that sun. *One Cloud Feels Lonely.* It occurred to her that it was one year to the day since she and Landon moved to Lowbone. She made a tiny sound in her throat that Harlon heard as a whimper. He touched her back and asked if she was okay.

She looked at the ground and nodded.

They walked beside one another and didn't say much the rest of the way into town. The spring birds sang their spring songs. Joy hummed quietly along.

The dog, Girl, glanced up at them as they went.

In the basement Landon moved the shelving unit. He took the key from around his neck and slipped it into the keyhole. He opened the steel door, flicked on the light, and entered the room. He sat at the table where he kept Joy's journal. He opened the journal and read a few pages.

He flipped to the end where he kept a few folded pages of his own. He opened and flattened them on the table. Picked up the pencil he kept beside the journal, sharpened to a point, and wrote the title of the novel he'd read the day before at the bottom of the numbered list. The title was only three letters long. He wrote it in all-caps, like on the cover. He had picked that novel because of the picture of the farmhouse on the front, and he liked the title: the old-fashioned word for enemy. He felt it was a suitable bookend, visually at least, to the first book he had read with the picture of the house and the truck on the front, by the sea. He looked at the list on the page in front of him. One hundred titles. One hundred was a good number.

He refolded the pages, which included the list of the things about Joy that he loved, and returned them to the back of the journal. He stood from the table and clutched the journal to his chest the way someone committed to spreading the good word might hold a well-worn copy of the Bible.

"It's been a long winter," he said, not only to himself. "I think I'm ready to see her again."

"Are you certain? It won't be easy to see her with him."

"Certainty's impossible. And I'm not after easy. I'm after Joy."

◆

A few days earlier, with signs of winter waning, Landon drove into town. He went to the train station and the bus depot to ask about Joy, but the attendants told him they were not at liberty to divulge information about anyone they might have sold tickets to. Of course. He understood. He thanked them and went to the grocery store for a few supplies. He placed the items on the conveyor belt for the clerk to scan.

"There's a woman with hair the colour of old wood. She has green eyes. She might be the most beautiful woman you have ever seen. I was wondering—"

The clerk looked over both shoulders and leaned toward Landon. "You should know. She took up with Harlon Glen."

"—."

"The man who runs The Wolf Den."

"—."

"I'm sorry to be the one to tell you. You seem like a nice man."

"No. I appreciate you telling me." Landon did his best to remain even. "I was wondering, do you ever see them? Here in town, I mean."

"They're at The Heather all the time. I don't think she cooks much."

Landon laughed and the clerk looked confused.

"No," Landon said. "No, she does not."

Landon took his bag of groceries and left the store. He climbed into the truck that once belonged to the man Joy had left him for. He drove home. He made a pot of coffee and listened to a record. He sat in the living room. He stared at the painting. He thought about his chickens and what else there was in his life to protect.

—◆—

Bill was at the counter when Harlon and Joy walked into The Heather and it was Joy who put a hand in the air and asked him to join them. They took the table by the window. Esther attended to them and commented on how good Joy looked.

"God above. When I was carrying mine I was as big as a fridge. Look at you. Perfect little beach ball, not an ounce anywhere else. When are you due?"

"The doctor says the middle of June but it feels like a month ago."

Joy touched the curve of her belly and looked at her hand there. Nothing had ever felt more real.

"Last stretch is always the hardest. You'll be fine."

Joy pressed her lips together and smiled.

Esther to Harlon. "Tell me you finally got off your wallet and bought this one a ring."

Harlon shook his head. "She ain't interested."

"Can't say I blame her."

Bill laughed.

Harlon made a serious face.

"Oh, don't look so glum. I'm only teasing. Now, what do you want?"

Harlon wanted a beer. He wanted a whisky. He wanted something. But he had promised Joy. He had promised her.

"Coffee. And whatever you've got dead and stuck between two slices of bread."

"Listen to him," Bill said. "The poet. Sounds so good I'll have the same."

Esther turned to Joy and waited.

What did she want. What. Did. She. Want.

—◆—

Landon had not been to The Heather since the day he and Joy came to Lowbone to look at The Hart Farm last spring. He parked the truck and crossed the road and stood a while at the foot of the wooden steps, staring at the front doors.

A boy walked by, rubbing an apple on the front of his shirt.

"What's wrong with you?"

Landon looked at the boy. "There's nothing wrong with me."

The boy shrugged and carried on, tearing an entire side from the apple in a single bite as he went.

—◆—

Harlon went to the counter to pay. From a tin he kept in his shirt pocket Bill pinched a bit of tobacco and stuffed it in his cheek. Then he stood from the table and offered Joy a hand, which she took.

When she looked at Bill he grinned, a fleck of tobacco on his lower lip. She wanted to ask him how he'd gotten the scar over his eye. She wanted to ask him why he was alone. She wanted to ask him if he'd ever been in love.

"A year ago today."

Bill looked at her.

"A year ago today I moved here from the city."

"Is that a fact."

"It feels like yesterday and a lifetime all at once."

"I wouldn't know about that. I don't think much about the days gone by, and I've never looked past the day after tomorrow at a single thing in my life."

◆

The dog lashed to the newel post outside The Heather lifted her head, aware of something in the air no human sense could ever attend to. Satisfied with the harmlessness of whatever had alerted her, the dog settled and sighed.

It was this little break in the stillness that caused Landon to notice the dog. He tilted his head at the animal and approached it. The dog ignored the scuffed boots in front of her until the man who was in them crouched and set a friendly hand on her head.

Landon scratched behind the dog's ear, which made the dog close her eyes and pant.

"You look exactly like a wolf." Landon didn't remember Harlon's dog from the day he and Joy visited The Wolf Den, and the dog didn't seem to remember him. "That's what I'd call you if you were mine. Wolf."

The two stayed like this for a while and then without notice the dog stopped panting. She averted her gaze from Landon and looked toward the door that was opening.

Landon stood and turned and saw Joy exiting The Heather with a man he recognized.

"Well, well." Bill spit a stream of tobacco juice into the dirt. "Look what we have here."

Joy touched Bill's shoulder. Landon watched her touch Bill's shoulder and wondered if the clerk at the grocery store had mistaken who Joy had left him for.

Landon and Joy did not acknowledge each other at first. It was difficult to know what to say. She liked the beard he had grown. He looked like a woodsier version of himself. *A woodsier Landon Wood.* The thought made her smile. Landon saw her smile but misunderstood the reason. He noticed the bump under her shirt, too, and, continuing his misapprehension, it did not occur to him even for a moment that the bump might have anything to do with him.

Bill folded his arms over his chest and assessed Landon. "You know, with that beard you sort of look like him."

Joy looked at Bill and wondered who he meant.

"Old Robert Hart. They say his ghost haunts the place."

Joy remembered being on the river in the canoe. Who she thought was Landon standing on the dock, and then not.

"Maybe that farm's rubbing off on you," Bill said. "Better watch or they'll find you in the barn one day too, blood all over, knife cocked in your hand, a finger to your lips."

Molly's journal. *There are stories of intruders. Of people you know, people you know very well. Slipping in through the bedroom door, standing at the foot of the bed, still, smirking, lips curled like a wolf in a dream. A shushing finger to those lips.*

The Heather doors opened. Harlon appeared and Landon felt a rage rise within.

Harlon stood beside Joy and pinched a single fry from the take-out container he held in one hand. He flipped the fry into his mouth and offered the contents to Joy, who passed, then Bill, who partook of a few fries himself. Bill spit another stream of tobacco juice into the dirt and managed to chew and swallow the fries without mixing the two things, something close to skill in the mechanics of what he did.

Harlon took another fry and ate it. "What seems to be the trouble?"

Landon looked at him. "No trouble here."

"Way you're standing there, hands pocketed like you don't care a lick when anyone with a set of eyes can tell you do, tells me otherwise."

"The way a man stands does not say anything. Hands though." Landon drew his hands from his pockets, seeming to examine them, squeezing them into fists. "Hands have great potential to communicate."

Joy took note. It was the kind of thing she had never heard Landon say. She liked it. There seemed to be a kind of wildness about him she had never seen before. What would he do? What was he capable of?

Harlon narrowed his eyes. He looked at Landon and called the dog. He tapped his thigh and the dog pushed herself to her feet. She padded away from Landon, glancing at him as she went up the steps to Harlon's side.

"You know," Harlon said. "There's nothing for you here."

Landon looked at Joy. "There's everything for me here."

Joy bit her bottom lip. She felt a flutter she could not help.

Harlon popped another fry in his mouth and smirked.

"Must be some lonely," Bill said. "Living at that old farm alone."

Landon looked at him. "I'm not alone."

Joy folded her arms over the bump and waited for Landon to continue.

"I bought two hens."

"Hah," Bill said. "You are some strange."

And beautiful, thought Joy.

Harlon snuffled and shook his head. He descended the steps and walked past Landon. Bill went with him and Joy followed a few steps behind. Landon noticed a thumb-sized smudge of paint, like a bruise, on her shoulder. He wanted with everything he had, with everything he was, to touch her shoulder there.

She stopped and looked at him. "It was good seeing you, Landon."

Good, he thought. Good.

She turned from him then and walked away.

◆

Landon stood in the road outside The Heather. He watched Bill drive away in his truck. He watched Harlon and Joy and the dog get smaller as they continued to walk farther and farther away. Pockets of dust lifted with the breeze and settled around him. After a while Harlon and Joy and the dog were so far in the distance they seemed not to move. If he called out to them now there was no way they'd hear him. He pretended to hold his rifle, the butt in his shoulder, one hand cradling the barrel, the other set calmly within the hollow of the lever. He set his cheek to the body of the invisible gun, the way the man had shown him, closed one eye, and sighted his mark. "Pshew," he whispered as he squeezed the invisible trigger and absorbed the invisible shock. As he went to his truck, Landon saw the name on the clean white page of his mind, a slow-motion bullet ripping through the body of it.

~~Harlon.~~

QUIET

—◆◆◆—

Six weeks later. The middle of June.

Early every morning before the sun rose Landon took his rifle to the porch and at a distance stood watch over the coop he'd made for his two hens down by the barn. Often it was coyotes that came creeping. Twice he'd seen a fox. Raccoons made regular appearances. Once, a wolf. The animals were always quiet and stealthy in their creeping. Usually, if he fired a shot, the ruined silence and the spray of dirt were enough to scare the hopeful marauders away, but three times the smell and the nervous clacking of the chickens coupled with the predators' instincts had been too great and they could not resist further pursuit. The shots in the dirt made the animals hop and regroup but not retreat. Three times, then, Landon found himself having to shoot to kill. To protect. He did not bury the bodies and he did not burn them. He did not believe they deserved the ceremony, considering what they were trying to do. Instead, he stuffed the bodies of the animals he had shot in a bag and put them out with the trash.

After the sun had risen and the hens were safe, Landon stowed the rifle by the back door and went to the coop to collect the eggs. Outside the coop was a wooden sign he had carved two words into and affixed to a cedar post driven into the ground. Every morning he touched the sign and said the words to himself like a prayer. *Kalm Wood*. One of the hens he named Joy, the other Sorrow. He said hello to Joy and Sorrow when he collected the eggs. He carried the eggs back to the house where he cracked them into a glass, gave them a single stir, and drank them down.

—◆—

It was quiet at The Wolf Den.

Joy spent a lot of time in the room she used as a studio, painting skies. Sometimes she sat in the chair by the window, reading, thinking, looking out. Sometimes she wrote in Molly's journal. She was thinking a lot about what Bill had said. How Landon's beard made him look like Robert Hart. How Robert Hart had done something terrible. How maybe the place was rubbing off on Landon. She worried about him. She wanted him to be okay.

Harlon was busy working. He was tired at night and in the morning and he was quiet all the time. Before she came here last winter she had imagined him quiet. She had imagined him rugged and hard-working and able and protective and strong. And he was. He was all of these things. But in her imagining she had added layers that turned out not to be there. Adding layers was the artist in her. Adding layers, though, she knew, altered things. Adding layers always changed a thing into something it was not.

—◆—

Landon had driven to The Wolf Den six times, once a week, and parked under the sign. Each time he went it was after midnight. Each time he went he killed the headlights as he turned onto the Glen Road and crept toward the driveway. He sat there for an hour in the truck in the dark, staring through the windshield up at the house. He pictured Joy lying next to Harlon, one of her hands touching him as they slept, the life within her growing and kicking and wanting in its own inarticulable way to be free.

He spoke to the empty cab of the truck in a voice not quite his own.

"You need to protect what is yours."

He shook his head once. "Joy is not something to possess."

"That's not what I mean. I mean the thing you had with her. Your life."

"Yes." Landon's eyes fell to the rifle in the passenger seat. "Our life."

DUE

—◆◆◆—

It was late. Joy walked into the living room and found Harlon asleep in the chair. She was wearing one of his plaid shirts. There were black and violet and burnt orange smudges on it. She had been painting another sky.

The dog sensed Joy and lifted her head.

Harlon opened his eyes.

Joy set a hand to her mouth. She was crying.

Harlon stood and held her. She let herself fall into him, her face against his chest. He held the back of her head. She felt safe. She appreciated that he didn't ask her why she was crying. She appreciated that he didn't pretend to understand.

She took a deep breath and sighed and forced herself to stop crying. She muttered something into his chest. He could feel the words against him. He took her face in his hands and looked at her. He waited and she repeated what she'd said.

"The baby, Harlon. The baby isn't yours."

He did not mean to hurt her, but when the deeply rooted evolutionary pangs of jealousy and the attendant rage rose within him—something he had in his whole life never felt to this extent—he bit down hard and every muscle in his body tensed. Without knowing he was doing it, he squeezed Joy's face in his hands, hard enough that it scared her, effectively enough that she couldn't manage words. Joy clutched his wrists and tried to pull his hands away.

He saw the fear in her widened eyes and let go. He let go with the force and the suddenness of the brain finally getting its message to the hands: *if you do not let go this instant the thing you are holding will break.* The force and the suddenness of Harlon's letting go transferred to Joy's body and she fell. Harlon tried to catch her.

She stared up at him, eyes full of pain and disbelief and terror.

Harlon stepped towards her. She showed him a hand, shook her head once.

The whole scene lasted only a few seconds.

Harlon fell into his chair.

Joy made her way to her feet. She could still feel his hands on her face. She spread her fingers—like a wall, like a force field—across her belly.

It was at this moment she felt her water break.

—◆—

Beyond midnight, Landon turned onto the Glen Road and killed the headlights. He stopped the truck beneath the sign and stared at the house for exactly one hour. He looked at his father's watch at the end of the hour. He smelled the leather band and closed his eyes. He opened them and reached for the rifle in the passenger seat. He climbed down from the cab and walked, unhurried, up the driveway.

His mind was clear. When he ascended the porch steps he turned and he could see a version of himself and Joy standing close to the fire pit last spring, a wisp of smoke rising. He could see Harlon with the dog, standing there. He could hear Joy saying something about a pair of gloves. He could see her climbing the porch steps to where he was now. He could see the screen door snapping against the house in the breeze.

He reached for that screen door. He was wearing those gloves. He clutched the handle and the hinges creaked as he pulled. He heard a clicking on the wooden floor within and then barking. He waited for the lights in the window. Surely one of them would hear the dog and seek out the disturbance.

He waited. No lights turned on and no one came.

He held the screen door open with a knee and tried the main door. It was unlocked. He turned the knob and entered the house and closed the door behind him. The dog cowered but continued to bark. Landon set the butt of the rifle on the kitchen floor and knelt. He whispered to the dog that he wasn't there to hurt her. There was no need to worry. Everything was okay.

"Shhh." He set a soft hand on the animal's head. "Shhh."

The dog responded, quietened, settled. She recognized Landon's voice and his smell.

Landon stood and considered turning on a light, but then thinking of how far away a light in the darkness could be seen he decided against it. He made his way through the kitchen to the next room, the floorboards creaking beneath him.

The house felt strangely familiar. It was, in its design, almost the same as his own. He went to a room and opened the door. He wasn't surprised when he saw the canvases and the bookcase against one of the walls. He got close enough in the dark to look at the paintings and saw they were all paintings of the sky.

He left the room and went down the hall. He stood in front of what he knew must be the bedroom door. He listened for their breathing. Turning the knob as soundlessly as he could he pushed the door open. The bed was empty. He stepped inside. He wondered where they could be but then it occurred to him that Harlon's truck had not been outside. He had no experience with such things, but when he saw Joy in town six weeks previous she had looked like she was soon due.

Landon set the rifle against the wall and stepped to what he thought must be Joy's side of the bed. He picked up the pillow and buried his face in it. He inhaled and held the pillow there.

The dog started barking again and Landon heard a definite but muted click: the sound of a truck door being shut.

He replaced the pillow on the bed.

He turned and picked up the rifle.

The screen door creaked open and he heard someone enter the house.

Landon stepped into the hallway, levelling the gun.

NEW LIFE

—◆◆◆—

The next morning Landon arrived at the small country hospital just after visiting hours began. He approached the desk in the New Life Centre and, introducing himself as a close friend, inquired about Joy.

The nurse behind the desk smiled. "It was a long night, but mom and baby are doing well."

The words *mom* and *baby* made Landon's heart go and he asked if he could see them.

The nurse gave him the room number: 107.

"They're sleeping. But you can peek your head in and see. If you're quiet."

Landon walked, unhurried, down the corridor. He located the room and looked at the number. He tried to think why it felt so familiar.

He stood in the doorway, a bouquet of daisies in his hand.

The room was darkened by the closed blinds. Joy and the baby were sleeping. There were no sounds but their breathing.

He thought about what Joy had said when he saw her in front of The Heather. *It was good seeing you, Landon.* She could have said *nice* instead of *good. Nice* would have been different. She could have agreed with what Harlon had said, that there was nothing for him here. She could have not smiled. She could have said only *goodbye.* She could have said nothing at all. She could have not said his name. *Saying someone's name is significant,* the man who wore sweaters had told him during one of their sessions. *It helps us remember who they are.*

Landon stood in the doorway and whispered Joy's name. *Joy.*

—◆—

Landon returned to the nurses' desk and asked if they had a vase he could borrow. One of the nurses went away and returned with one. She handed the glass vase to him and he thanked her. She smiled and directed him to the waiting room. He would find a sink there and a pair of scissors to snip the ends.

Landon went to the waiting room. He filled the vase with water, then stood over the sink and snipped the daisy stems one at a time. He tore the plant food packet open with his teeth and watched the powder dissolve in the water. He stood the stems in the vase, pleased with his work.

Landon took the vase to Joy's room and walked in, careful not to wake her. He set the vase on the windowsill. If he opened the blinds, the sun would wake her. He left the blinds closed and went to the foot of the bed. He saw the baby, sleeping, and he looked at Joy.

He stood there.

He stood there and watched her sleep.

—◆—

Landon returned to the waiting room and made himself a coffee. He drank the coffee and then rinsed and dried the cup and stood it in the basket by the sink. He opened all the cupboards. In one he found a tea candle, a votive holder, and a lighter. He took the holder down and set the candle in it. He pocketed the lighter. He walked back to Joy's room and stood again in the doorway. He struck the flint wheel with his thumb, over and over and over again, inside his pocket, which warmed the space against his hand.

◆

When the baby woke the baby cried, and when the baby cried Joy's eyes opened. She brought herself to a sitting position with some discomfort on her face. A nurse pushed past Landon in the doorway and picked up the baby. Joy took the baby from the nurse and held him. He fit perfectly in her arms. The nurse watched for a moment, then left. Joy quietened the baby's crying with her touch. She fed him.

Landon entered the room and set the votive holder on the table beside the bed. He lit the candle. The blinds were still closed. The candle offered a little wavering light.

He sat in the chair by the bed and touched Joy's arm.

She looked at him and smiled. "Landon. I'm so glad it's you."

HOME

‑◆◆◆‑

The Hart Farm. One month later.

Luna was asleep at the foot of the bed in a crib Landon had made. Joy was asleep, too. Landon was in a chair by the bedroom window, looking out. The sun was low, the sky like rust.

He'd known she would come home. He'd known she would. And now, here she was.

‑◆‑

Later, Joy came into the kitchen, Luna asleep in his sling, and joined Landon at the table.

She asked him what he was doing.

"Sitting."

He reached out to touch the sling. He felt the infant's warmth coming through it.

"We're going to walk into town." Joy touched Luna's little head. He wriggled against her. She looked at Landon. "Maybe you can read to him later."

"I'd like that."

Joy touched Landon's arm.

He looked at her hand there. He put his own hand on top of hers. He did not want to let it go.

◆

Joy walked the country roads into town, the warm June sun
muted by a coven of white clouds. She approached the bookstore
and walked in. It had been such a long time since she'd been here.

The copper bell dinged as she entered. Rose came through
the beaded curtain, wiping her hands on a tea towel. She was
wearing a black woollen skirt. Her glasses were turquoise, as was
her blouse and her shoes.

Joy stood in front of the counter and bounced a sleeping
Luna in his sling.

Rose looked at the baby. "I had no idea."

"This is Luna."

Rose touched the baby's nose. "Hello, little Luna. Aren't
you precious."

Joy looked at Rose. "He is. That's exactly the word."

Rose continued to admire the sleeping baby. The two
women were quiet for a while. Dove, the cat, was on the
windowsill. He stretched and dropped to the floor. On his way
by, the cat brushed Joy's shins and continued his quiet walk
through the curtain in the back.

Rose watched the cat go, then turned again to Joy. "I have
something for you."

Rose went to a shelf filled with colourful books and
returned with one in her hand. The cover was a picture of a room
with a fireplace and a window. On the mantel was a clock. Above
the fireplace was a painting of a cow jumping over the moon.
Framed by the window, the actual moon and the stars.

Joy read the title out loud.

"It's perfect." She looked at Rose. "Thank you."

"So. The winter that comes has come and gone."

"It has."

"Not without its difficulties."

Joy smiled, her lips together, and shook her head once.

"Well, little siren. You seem happy."

"I am."

"You seem like you found what you were looking for."

Joy looked down at Luna. She looked at Rose and thumbed her eyes.

"I think I found what I didn't know I was looking for."

—◆—

After she left the bookstore, Joy went to the grocer. She wondered what she would say if she ran into Harlon. She wondered what he would say. Telling him the baby wasn't his was the beginning of the end of things. She knew that. But how could he have hurt her the way he did? He hadn't meant to, she was sure, but that wasn't the point. The point was he was capable of it. Until that moment she had not seen even the remotest possibility of him hurting her and she did not know how she had missed it.

Luna was still asleep. Joy loved the feel of him cinched tightly against her in the sling. She loved the growing heft of him. The little sounds he made when he slept. When he whimpered she felt something alive at the base of her neck. There was nothing else like it in the world.

One day it would be the last day she held him this close. The last day he wore these little socks. This little shirt. The last day he looked at his own fist like it was the greatest discovery in the history of the world. One day it would be the last day she drew him this close in the sling and she would not know it. The sling would go in a box and if she ever opened that box the sling would look and feel like an artifact from another time. If she picked it up and smelled it it would not smell like the baby him. It would not smell like him at all. If nostalgia encouraged her to sling the sling around her shoulders all she would feel was the emptiness where the baby him no longer rested. The baby him would no longer exist outside of pictures. Outside her mind.

Joy saw the baby him in a painting.

Luna in a Sling.

Joy walked with her grocery basket through the produce section. She stopped and picked an avocado from the bin and tested its firmness. The dark green was beginning to blacken. Soon it would be perfect. Left too long it would turn to mush inside and look like a dead thing. Now, though, it looked and felt like a dinosaur egg. What Joy imagined a dinosaur egg would look and feel like. Long ago there was the last dinosaur egg and no dinosaur knew it.

She picked up a few other items and went to the cash. The girl who rang her through fussed over Luna. When she left the store the sun was still a bright force in the sky. She shielded her eyes against it. She thought of the paintings she had done of the sky and had left at Harlon's. She wondered if he would mind her coming to pick them up.

◆

Landon had listened to The Fortunate Ones sing "The Bliss" ten times in a row. It's not that he could relate, so much, to the story the singers were telling, but certain lines stuck out to him and he liked the chorus. The song's last lines seemed to fit the way he was feeling these days. He had a good heart and able hands. He had Joy again and their son.

Harlon's name never came up. Landon knew she must think about him. He had read her journal, after all, more than once, which he still kept in the basement in the room behind the secret door. He thought it was fitting that he kept it down there. The day Joy found Molly's journal in the box she had dreamed of, Landon was sitting at the small table in the room behind the secret door. At that particular moment only the door separated them. He heard her rummaging around the shelves where he had found the hammock and the key on the leather string. It hadn't take him long to rig up a system that pulled the shelves back into place when he pulled the door closed and sat in the room. He could hear Joy striking the little lock on the box with the wrench. He heard her struggle to separate the chairs. He heard the silence after and pictured her sitting there under the small window, the light slipping in. He did not know at the time what she was doing, so he waited. He looked at Molly, sitting across from him in the chair she had been sitting in for twenty years, her bony wrists lashed to the table with leather straps.

"That's who you were telling me about, isn't it," Landon said, in a voice not quite his own.

"Yes. That's Joy. I don't know what she's doing. She never comes down here."

"Are you going to tell her about me?"

"No," he said. "No, I don't think that I am."

—◆—

Landon did not visit the room behind the secret door in the basement as much these days. Now that Joy was home. But he had visited Molly every day throughout the winter when he was alone. They talked. He enjoyed their talks. Talking with her had a calming effect. He told her about Joy. He told her about himself. He told her about his parents. How there was no doubt in his mind the accident had been his fault. If he had not needed the help his parents believed he needed and wanted him to get then they would still be here.

Landon told Molly that the green stones in the bracelet she was wearing reminded him of the colour of Joy's eyes, and the thin bead of copper that encased the stones reminded him of the colour of her hair. He was so happy Joy was home again. He was so happy he could look into those eyes and smell that hair.

—◆—

After listening to "The Bliss" for the tenth time, Landon stood and turned the record player off. He replaced the album in its sheath and returned it to its spot near the beginning of the first of the seven shelves. He checked the needle and wiped the turntable. When he was finished, he left the house and walked down to the barn. He opened the door and entered the barn and walked over and unhooked the rope that brought down the steps leading to the attic that used to be the mow. He had made it another space in which he could work. He climbed the steps and turned on the light and looked at the wooden statue of Joy he'd been carving since January. He touched the statue's face. It was a good likeness. He was nearly finished.

He folded his arms and took a deep breath and held it.

After a while he checked his father's watch, descended the steps, and pulled the rope that returned the steps to their hiding place, flush with the ceiling.

He exited the barn and touched the sign in front of the coop and said the words. *Kalm Wood.* He opened the gate and walked inside the run. The hens flitted about and clucked, which Landon always interpreted as them saying hello.

"Hello. How are you both? There's no need to worry now. My heart—it's okay."

UNDER THE SKIES
& SOMEWHERE DEEP IN THE DARK

‑◆◆◆‑

Joy put Luna down for his nap and walked into the kitchen to find Landon at the table with a coffee, reading.

Landon looked up.

Joy folded her arms and assessed the unfamiliar scene.

Landon took a drink of his coffee and set the mug down. "I read now."

"I see that."

"I read a lot of your books. When you were gone. I hope you don't mind."

"Of course not." She pictured him reading her books. She hadn't been able to find her old journal. Now she knew. No more secrets.

Joy picked up Landon's mug and warmed her hands with it. She took a sip. She set the mug down and picked up the truck keys.

Landon watched her.

"I have to go get some things."

"—."

"If Luna wakes up, there's a bottle in the fridge."

"—."

"Are you okay?"

"As ever I have been."

Joy tucked her hair. She turned on a heel and left. Landon returned to his book.

—◆—

Bill hadn't seen or heard from Harlon in a while. It wasn't uncommon for a couple of weeks to go by, a month sometimes, without seeing or talking to him, but it had been longer than that. He had a bad feeling.

Bill got in his truck and drove to Harlon's, just to see.

At first, everything seemed normal. Harlon's truck was gone, which meant he'd likely taken off somewhere. He did that sometimes. Bill knew from Esther that Joy had gone back to the city boy, that the baby wasn't Harlon's. There was no doubt in Bill's mind, when he thought about it, that Harlon had likely gone on a tear.

Bill clomped up the porch steps. There was a bit of dirt on the porch boards below the kitchen window. He investigated and saw that something had been digging around in the flowerpot that sat on the brick windowsill. A squirrel, likely, looking for something that wasn't there. Bill didn't think much of it. He let himself into the house.

He flicked on the light. What he saw stopped him dead. He went no farther. After a time, he cleared his throat, turned, and pulled the door closed behind him.

What he saw, what he left there curled in the corner of the kitchen, were the emaciated remains of Girl, the dog. Patches of fur on her legs were gone. Something had taken her eyes and one of her ears was lacerated and hanging.

Bill clomped down the porch steps and back to his truck. He climbed into the cab and turned the key and thought to himself, Harlon never leaves that dog alone.

Bill peeled away like he was in a hurry. The tires spit old stones into the grass.

Beyond the grass, somewhere deep in the woods, was a shell casing no one would ever see. Eventually it would sink into the ground and remain buried there forever. Like the secret it belonged to.

Landon, not only to himself

I'm going to miss you.

You were right not telling anybody.

I think so.

Some things need to stay hidden so that other things can be found.

That's a good way to look at it.

I see you have something there.

Yes. A pinecone. I've had this one for a long time. It used to hang from the rearview mirror in my parents' car. I'd like to leave it here. If that's okay. I think it will help me finally move on if I know it's safe here with you.

Moving on is important.

It is. Yes.

Take good care of yourself, Landon.

Thank you, Molly. I will.

Joy, in Molly's journal

When I went to Harlon's to get my paintings
I sensed something was wrong even before I
turned onto the Glen Road. Sometimes you get a
feeling that's stronger than knowing and there's no
explaining it.

The door was locked. Harlon never locked
the door. He told me once where he kept the key
in case I locked myself out. I dug around in the
flowerpot on the windowsill until I found the key
he'd buried there.

The sight and the smell when I opened the
door hit me at once. My hands went to my mouth
and I gasped. I shielded my eyes from the sight
in the corner and went to the spare room and
collected the paintings as quickly as I could.

The bedroom door was closed. I wanted to
go in, but I didn't know what I might find. My
curiosity got the better of me. I reached for the
handle and stepped inside.

When the phone rang Joy knew it was Cynthia before she picked up.

"Hello, my dear. Do you know why I'm calling?"

"You're looking for a show."

"Have you been working?"

"Yes and no. I don't have as much time these days."

"There is as much time in any given day now as there has always been."

Joy smiled. She liked Cynthia. She really did.

"Things are different."

"Things."

"Landon and I have a son."

"A child. Well. What do people say? Congratulations?"

"Some people do."

Luna whimpered. For a moment his suckling quickened. Joy touched his nose and he looked up at her. "Why don't you make the drive from the city one afternoon. We'll have lunch. I'll show you the skies I've been working on."

"Skies."

"Mm hmn."

"You have me worried. But we shall see. Tell Landon we'll need another run of easels."

"He'll need a number."

"Twelve. Which is what I'll be looking for from you as well. Expect me in a month. We'll have lunch. I'll have a look at your skies."

"I look forward to it."

"There is no other way to look."

They said goodbye and Joy returned the phone to its cradle. As she did, she heard something in the basement. She stood with Luna and rebuttoned her shirt. She went to the top of the stairs and called Landon's name. He didn't answer. When she called a second time he appeared at the bottom step.

"What was that noise?"

He looked up at her, hands pocketed. "I didn't hear anything."

Joy furrowed her brow. She walked away from the top of the stairs and Landon began ascending them. He held the rail with one hand and kept the other in his pocket, feeling the smooth stones of the bracelet he had only moments ago liberated from Molly's wrist.

—◆—

Bill was in The Heather working on his third whisky and he asked Esther to borrow the phone. She clutched the old-fashioned unit like a bowling ball and dropped it with a ding on the counter in front of him. Then she left him alone.

Bill set the receiver to his ear and spun the number on the dial. Three rings. Then a click.

"Pine Realty."

"Marty. Bill here."

"Bill. How are things?"

"Good. Listen. I'll get right to it. You're the one sold the old Hart farm last year. Am I right?"

"You are."

"I got to ask—did you notice anything funny about the one you sold it to?"

Marty thought about it. "No. I wouldn't say so. Not really. Why?"

"I don't know. Don't matter, I guess. Say, you seen Harlon around lately?"

"Can't say as I have."

"Haven't heard from him in a while. Went out to his place and found his dog dead in the kitchen. Been dead a while."

"That's no good. Sorry to hear that."

"Yeah. Well. He never went too far without that dog."

"People do strange things sometimes."

"I suppose they do."

"You know it's funny you should mention the one who bought the Hart farm. I heard the missus took up with Harlon over the winter."

"She did. A real peach, that one."

"Sure. She seemed it."

"I don't know what happened with her and Harlon but she went back to the city boy."

"That so."

"Yep."

"Well. Sorry I couldn't be of more help, Bill."

"Ain't nobody can help me, Marty."

"Hah. True for us all. We'll see you, Bill."

"See you, Marty."

Bill hung up the phone and took a pull off his whisky.

Esther returned, drying a glass. "What was that about?"

"Nothing. You haven't seen Joy in here lately, have you?"

"Not since she had the baby. Why?"

"Worried about Harlon is all. Haven't heard from him in a while."

"Likely on a tear. Went on the wagon there for what, six months. He's due for a good one."

"You're probably right." Bill finished his drink. "Esther."

"Bill."

He dropped some money on the counter and left.

Landon, to his son sleeping in the cradle

Everything is good now.

—

People pick up and leave without a word all the time. He's done it before.

—

Don't worry. No one will find his truck.

—.

No one goes into the woods that far. I was an hour walking back.

—

The body won't be there.

—

I heard the wolves. They were snarling. They were hungry.

—

Yes. Everything's settled. And *settled* is the word.

Landon and Joy sat on the porch with the record player and a monitor broadcasting the sleeping sounds of their son. Landon opened the bottle of Valpolicella he'd been saving and poured two glasses. He set the bottle down on the wrought iron table Joy had taken from her apartment in the city.

He held up his glass. "To our family."

"I shouldn't."

"I didn't give you too much."

She picked up her glass. "Sometimes too much is barely enough."

Landon recognized the line. He thought about it and the author's name came to him. He told Joy.

She took a sip, shrugged her eyes. "I'm impressed."

He took a sip, shrugged his shoulders. "Like I said, I read a lot of your books."

Joy set her glass on the table. Landon set his next to hers. So close they almost touched.

"I have something for you."

He stood and went to the record player. He put on the album he had picked for the occasion. Springsteen's *Darkness on the Edge of Town*.

He returned to the table and sat. He held out his palm.

Joy looked at the wooden ring resting there. She took it and slid it on the pinky finger of her right hand and turned it with her thumb.

He watched her. He wished he could tell what she was thinking.

"I have something else."

He reached under his chair and produced a small wooden box he had made and handed it to her. Joy opened it. She gasped and touched her chest. She looked at him.

"It's beautiful."

She took the bracelet out of the box and put it on.

"It belonged to someone very special."

Joy didn't ask who. She assumed he meant his mother.

She reached across the table. Landon took her hand and stood. She stood with him and set her face against his chest. He kissed her forehead. They danced on the spot, barely moving, while Springsteen sang "Something in the Night."

In the distance, a truck was coming down Hart Road. Landon saw it. He watched it turn up their driveway. It was getting dark and the truck's headlights were on.

"Are you expecting someone?"

"No."

Joy looked. She recognized the truck.

"It's Bill." She felt her stomach drop.

Landon undid Joy's arm from his waist. "That will be my exit then."

"Stay."

Landon looked at the darkening sky. He looked at Joy. Then he went in the house and the screen door snapped shut behind him.

Joy turned the record player off and stood at the top of the steps, arms folded, like she was cold.

The truck rolled to a stop. Bill turned it off and climbed out. He closed the door. At the bottom of the steps he stopped and looked up at her. "There's a peach."

She smiled. "It's good to see you, Bill."

"It's good to be seen."

Joy glanced over her shoulder. Bill came up the steps and they sat together at the table.

"So. Where's the city boy?"

"He's not a city boy anymore, Bill."

"Uh huh."

They sat a while, not saying anything. Then without precedent or warning Joy reached across the table and traced three fingers down the length of the scar over Bill's left eye. The way someone might touch ancient markings on a cave wall, curious but not wanting not to hurt or disturb or disrespect the markings themselves.

She let her fingers linger at the bottom of the scar. "I always wanted to know—what happened here."

"A wolf."

Joy pulsed her eyes. "Really. You're lucky."

Bill understood what Joy meant, but something about how she said it made what she said sound a little like envy, too.

He lit a cigarette. Took a deep pull and blew the smoke over his shoulder. He seemed to be looking at something in the distance.

"I haven't seen or heard from Harlon in a while. Went out to the house." He looked at her and stopped himself from telling her about the dog. "Truck was gone. Esther figures he's on a tear."

"I don't know if he ever told you, but he used to talk a lot about just picking up one day and leaving. Sometimes he sounded really serious about it. He said he wanted me to go with him." She shrugged. "Maybe he finally did it."

Bill looked at her. He didn't know what had happened between them, but he knew things had ended badly. Maybe Joy was right. Maybe this time Harlon was gone for good. But the dog. Why wouldn't he have taken the dog?

"Anyway. I should go. Just wanted to stop by to say hey, and congratulations."

"Thank you. I wish—"

Bill placed a hand on the table and looked at her. "Don't wish."

Joy walked with Bill to the top of the steps. She slipped her hands in her back pockets and watched him make his way to his truck.

He showed her a hand, climbed into the cab, and drove away. She watched the truck go. She watched the dust rise in the truck's wake. She took note of how the dust seemed to hang there in the dusklight. Like the tiny pixels of a spectre, disappearing. The sky itself was moments from going dark. She would paint this sky. It would be the final sky in her series of skies. She thought of a line from *Wide Sargasso Sea:* "I turned and saw the sky. It was red and all my life was in it." The line gave her the title for the painting, for the whole series. *All My Life.*

———◆———

Landon had been sequestered inside the house, watching from the kitchen window. When he saw the truck drive away he rejoined Joy on the porch. He stood beside her, arms folded.

"What did he want?"

"To say hey, and congratulations."

Joy looked at Landon. She looked at his eyes. She looked in and around them, like she had just now found something there. She pictured him inside Harlon's house, inside the bedroom. She could see him straightening the sheets, fluffing the pillows, setting the pinecone on the bedside table. She would never ask him about what he had done. It didn't bother her and she wondered why. She wondered what not being bothered by it meant.

"I was thinking," he said. "I would like to finish the basement. Nothing fancy. Frame and drywall the walls. Put down a floor."

Joy grinned. "How very House of Usher of you."

Inside their bedroom Luna woke and started crying. They could hear him through the monitor on the table.

Joy tucked her hair. She patted Landon's chest. "I better go check on our son."

Alone, Landon walked over to the porch rail and clutched it with both hands. He breathed in and held it.

"*The only way to really keep something close to your heart*," the man who wore sweaters once told him, prophet that he was, "*is to picture a clean white page in your mind and think of the words.*"

Luna, Landon thought. Our son.

Two words appeared on the clean white page in his mind.

Moon.

Sun.

The actual sun had slipped below the horizon like someone slipping unannounced from a room. The actual moon was hanging in the sky, in the dark, like a ghost.

Somewhere deep in the night a wolf stands by a truck, still as a painting, eyes locked on something only it can see. The wolf pins a clean white bone in its paws to the ground. The wolf might bury the bone. If it doesn't, the woods themselves will bury it in time. In a thousand years someone will unearth the bone and document the length and the girth and calculate the age and speculate about the teeth marks. In a thousand years, science will be able to recreate the man the bone belonged to. Science by then may well be able to dissect all the mysteries that lurk in the dark. It may well be able to tell us everything we want to know about the people we love. About love itself. How many things we never see. How many things we never really understand. In a thousand years someone might find the bone, and tell a story.

ACKNOWLEDGMENTS

With much appreciation & gratitude…

to Transatlantic agent & editor extraordinaire

Evan Brown—
all around fine fellow without whom this book would not
be a book—more specifically, for the tireless (re)reading,
suggesting, editing, & continual genuine support

to the readers who read the various iterations

Stephanie Sinclair—
for the initial encouragement & the chance & for helping to
bring Evan on board

Bethany Gibson—
for the real, honest feedback that helped me see Landon &
Joy clearly, not to mention the story to which they belong

Naben Ruthnum—
for the conversation about *Your Life Is Mine*, one of the
novels that inspired the short story "Nightsounds" & led to
the first draft; for taking the time (when you were no doubt
short on time) to read & offer such a thoughtful comment

to Signature Editions

Doug Whiteway—
for saying yes & all the fine edits & suggestions

Karen Haughian—
for helming the ship & the correspondence & all the attention
to the process

Ashley Nielsen—
for all the fine detailing & hard work

to Blue Heron Books

Shelley Macbeth (et al.)—
for the boundless, ongoing support & opportunity...I'm
without the words

to the family in the country without whom I would be lost in the dark

Mom—
for every single thing you have always done & continue to
do; for every single thing you have always been & continue
to be

Stacy, Justin, Carys, Brynn—
no one can ever know how much the four of you mean to the
five of us, aside from the four of you & the five of us

Powell—
for all of the help at the house & in the garden & with the
chickens; for all the conversations

Ethan, Penelope, Abigael—
for listening to the old man yammer on & for all of your
ideas...everything you are & do fills my heart with all the
good things I can name, not least of which is knowing I get
to call myself your dad

Tara—
for suggesting this little life, for keeping it afloat, for all the
love, for all the things that make us us

DARYL SNEATH

Daryl Sneath is an author and high school English and Philosophy teacher from rural Ontario. He is the author of three novels, *In the Country in the Dark*, *As the Current Pulls the Fallen Under*, and *All My Sins*. Daryl holds an MA in Literature & Creative Writing from The University of Windsor. His poetry and fiction have been published in journals including *The Antigonish Review*, *Prism international*, *Wascana Review*, *Nashwaak Review*, *paperplates*, *Zouch Magazine*, *Quilliad*, *FreeFall*, *Filling Station*, *The Dalhousie Review*, and *The Literary Review of Canada*. One of his short stories was longlisted for the CBC Short Story Prize.

Eco-Audit
Printing this book using Rolland Enviro100 Book
instead of virgin fibres paper saved the following resources:

Trees	Water	Air Emissions
1	1,000 L	207 kg